WITCH WAY DID HE GO?

BETTINA M JOHNSON

AQUA RAVEN PUBLISHING

Witch Way Did He Go?

ISBN: 978-1-7350692-4-1(paperback)

Cover art by StunningBookCovers.com

❀ Created with Vellum

For my dad, Salvatore, who always inspires with his work ethic.
You gave me all I ever needed to succeed.

CHAPTER 1

"**F**or as long as I live, I will never understand men!"

I tossed a paint rag across my workspace. It just missed landing in the bin I use to hold all the dirty items awaiting wash day. Scowling at my blunder, I shuffled over to the offending cloth, picked it up off the floor, and shoved it into the basket.

My cousin and best friend, Andrea, giggled uncontrollably at my outburst. She organized my supply tray and won the battle against a mass of tangled paperclips I used to hold pieces of fabric to my sculpture. I'm a mixed media artist. I find everyday items, mostly someone else's junk—metal pipes, gears and cogs, and other oddities—and would turn them into my kind of treasure. I'd weld them, paint them and create useful pieces of working art; bird feeders, whirligigs, wind chimes, rain chimes, and yard art.

"You aren't supposed to understand men. Just forgive them for not having the superior intellect and witchy wisdom we women possess in abundance. Let's face it. We keep them around for two things...one of which is spider removal."

I gave Andrea a droll look then sniffed. "I suspect they know we will take over doing whatever it is they pretend to be clueless at...they count on it even. Playing dumb gets them out of work." I slammed my hand down on the table that held my art supplies for emphasis, only to have the container with my paintbrushes tip over onto the floor, scattering the contents. I made the motion to kick at the can but thought better of it, gathering them up instead, and replaced them where they'd rested before my tantrum.

"But that isn't what I'm upset about. I am angered with this, 'let the Council handle things and go about making your art,' or 'you are just making things worse by fighting with the Elders, don't talk out of turn in public,' that he has been spouting recently, not that we've been out in public recently. Like I give two figs about outdated protocol and ridiculous laws that get us nowhere. Time is passing, and the Council's greatest concern is getting through heaps of red tape. I'll craft them a knife so sharp it will slice through miles of the stuff in seconds. He should be on my side when it comes to this matter."

"And just what has Lorcan done to bring down your wrath, thusly? I mean, I assume you are speaking about Lorcan unless another male is orbiting your witchy amazingness that you haven't told me about yet. Has he stopped you from presenting your list of grievances to the Council? Is he forbidding you from arguing your point?"

"No. And you better believe we are speaking of that...that..."

"Hey, Lily. I'm going out for lunch. Oh! Hey Andrea. Can I get you ladies something to eat?"

Speak the Devil's name, and he shows up.

I crossed my arms and glared at the man who ignored my expression, giving me a sideways hug, but not much else. I remained immobile and unaffected by his yummy man pine-scent, mixed with grease from working on cars, and an earthy fragrance. I may have possibly leaned into him slightly as my knees went weak. What? I can't help that I'm attracted to the man who is a walking thermostat that can make all your troubles go away with one touch.

Lorcan is an empath witch who can calm the worst panic attack or settle the nerves of a death row inmate with a pat on the head. Well, at least I believed he could. It's not that he's ever had the opportunity to try that one out. But I digress.

My name is Lily Sweet, the newest dark witch to grace the charmingly southern town of Sweet Briar, Georgia, with her presence. You heard me correctly. I said witch. Our town is a haven for witch folk with many ancient families living in and around our village nestled in the North Georgia mountains, with a few just over the border in North Carolina, as well. Seriously. If you are standing in some parts of our county and throw a rock, it will land in our sister state to the north.

Ours is a village of touristy schtick and artist colony boho combined with enough magical oddities to keep visitors enchanted—and coming back over and over again. Especially since we have a plethora of festivals for all to enjoy throughout the year, it just so happens we are still in the winter doldrums and have nary a festival in sight, which is perfect for my plans—no distractions to keep me from my task.

My task is figuring out a way to release my mother from her imprisonment and go forth to rescue my father from evil asshats who might be holding him against his will somewhere in the Pacific Northwest. Yeah. Goals. Gotta love them!

I just experienced the shock of a lifetime when my great-grandmother revealed her suspicions that my devious black cat, Wicked, was somehow fused with my mother, Aunt Adelaide. Oh, that came out wrong. You see, I just found out my mother, the woman I thought was my mother, Jessica Croy, was my aunt, and my Aunt Adelaide is, in fact, my birth mother! Why my father Charlie and the sisters, Jessica and Adelaide, felt the need to conceal this from the family is still a mystery. One we hope to reconcile when we release Adelaide from her feline prison—or find my dad.

I did not know of any of this because my mother, or Aunt Jessica, rather, took off with me after Adelaide, my mother, ran away to parts unknown, fearing an attack of some sort by an evil entity. When Adelaide left, my father, Charlie, went searching for her and instructed Jessica to abscond with me, go into hiding until he sent word that all was well. Word never came, as Charles Sweet seemingly disappeared as had Adelaide. I lived with Jessica, who I came to know as my mother, until she died of cancer last summer, leaving me instructions to head 'back home' to Sweet Briar, Georgia.

Surreal. I know. Trust me. I am just as gobsmacked with this as the rest of my family.

We now realize Adelaide is stuck in some magical body meld with my cat, Wicked, and I, for one, am concerned for their safety. What if separating the two means one or both should come to harm—even die? I might have a cantankerous relationship with that furball of mine, but the last thing I want is to see her eradicated by some horrid reversal spell. Although, at the rate any of us are going, it might take months, if not years, to figure out what dire magic was used to bind them together.

Even Adriana, my great-grandmother, the matriarch of

the Dolce clan and one of the most powerful dark witches out there, has not a clue as to what manner of witchcraft and spell-making were used on the pair least; I didn't think she did. And if she doesn't know, I am not sure there is a witch alive that does. Well, except for Donna Fredricks and her younger sister Deanna—the two witches who planned this attack on my family for reasons only their diabolical and deranged brains could comprehend.

And that, right there, is one of my tasks and yet another hurdle to cross. Donna is in an undisclosed witch prison, and we have been refused an audience with her thus far. We've been denied an audience because Adriana thinks we needn't tell the Elders of our discovery just yet, so they see no reason our family should know the whereabouts of the murderous witch. And Deanna? Well, Deanna is dead.

Donna confessed to killing her in a fit of evil, hide-protection, brilliance. Both she and Deanna performed some vile magic. Why keep a witness around in the form of one younger, and apparently troublesome sibling, when Donna could be rid of her and be the last baddie standing, so to speak? They did a snow job on this town, those two, that's for sure, before Donna betrayed her kin. All of the witch folk in my village had no idea the strength these two possessed. They never registered their true talents with the Council, convinced they were lessor witches.

The only thing we still cannot figure out is where Donna disposed of Deanna's body. Because the skeleton I'd discovered hidden under the porch at my home, which we assumed was Deanna Fredricks, turned out to be that of a missing teenager from Otto, North Carolina, after the authorities matched the dental records.

So where is Deanna's remains, then? I just hoped another skeleton wouldn't show up at my place and be hers!

Ever since the revelation that someone had possessed a

teen girl named Rowan Nightingale and had her murder our town's librarian, Edith Plank, tying it to my family, and the evil witch sister duo, the Council has been supposedly investigating heavily into the why of it all.

I knew three Elders, Tanaquil Alessi, Gloria Stillwell, and Olivia Ogden-Meyers, had been diligently researching this, informing us of any discoveries. My Aunt Chiara, who was a Dolce, my father's side of the family, and my Uncle Owen, married to my Aunt Iona, a Croy, and my mother's side, were both Elders as well—and they were making separate inquiries.

"No. I do not want lunch. Unless, of course, you'd like to take me out to Joe's? You know. Where we share a booth, and you and I could have a conversation? We could even bring Andrea along."

"Hey!" groused Andrea, then tossed a paperclip at me. It landed in my hair. I chose to ignore it.

Lorcan looked sheepish and eyed Andrea for some support. He found it, and I decided right then, and there I disliked them both. On a basic level, that is, since some part of me understood Lorcan's reticence at telling the world we were a couple and cautioning me not to antagonize the Council since they would hear our petitions soon enough. I figured he thought we already had enough on our plate to have our families distracted by our dating.

Whatever.

"We'll have what you're having, Lorcan. Keep it simple." Andrea stated, then gave me a wide-eyed look to say, 'cut the guy some slack.' I am not one for slack-cutting, however.

"I still don't know why we..."

"Hey, that's great. I will run to Joe's and get us some sandwiches and a cup of his minestrone. It is chilly out there." Lorcan rushed out of my art studio, cutting me off and leaving me even more disgruntled than I was before he wandered in on his lunch gathering mission.

"You can run, buster...but you can't hide from me. Or keep refusing to give me a solid reason as to why we need to keep this...this...whatever the heck we have going on, a secret." I yelled at his retreating back.

Andrea reeled back in shock, mouth agape, then sputtered a question.

"You mean, he hasn't told you why you need to keep things on the low down for now?"

I peered at my cousin in confusion as I replied, "I just assumed he didn't want his folks to fuss or have my aunts get all in his business and start in on the, 'so when will you two set a date?' stuff. I know I want to enjoy dating and get to know each other better before any mention of marriage or commitment scares the big goof away. I mean, we haven't even gone out on one date, let alone one where the town could take a gander at us and set the gossip mill off and running. Why am I now afraid to hear the real reason he is acting weird?"

"Oh...Lily. I am so sorry. Yet again, we fail you as a family. I keep forgetting how new to our witchy world you are. You see, dating isn't the issue. But before witch families sanction a serious commitment, couples, in this case, you and Lorcan need to go through The Tribunal."

"Oh...well, that is fine. We...wait. What?"

* * *

"WHEN WAS anyone around here going to inform me, I had no choice in a marriage partner?" I steadfastly refused to take the sandwich Lorcan had brought for me, so he gave up and put it on the desk in my office loft before heading back downstairs and next door to the safety of his mechanic shop. Andrea was trying to appear unobtrusive and tiny, sitting in her chair, barely making slurping sounds as she consumed her hot soup.

I turned to her, raising my brows, letting her know that I expected an answer in no uncertain terms. Sighing, she straightened up and placed her bowl down on the corner of my desk.

"Lily, you have a choice... it's not like that. However, if you guys are heading toward marriage and Lorcan would rather not have the world know that yet, he has reasons. He will tell them to you, I'm sure. Has it even gotten that serious yet? I mean, has Lorcan asked you to marry him?"

"Of course, he hasn't asked me to marry him! As I said, we haven't even gone out on a date yet! We don't know if we are truly compatible or if this is just some weird attraction that will fizzle out when I find out he snores, and he finds out I kick out in my sleep." Although how we were going to get to that revelation in light of our not going anywhere or doing anything was beyond me.

"When did he start acting different and get weird about being seen in public with you? I mean, it's not like him. And he obviously cares because...well, he just does! So, what has changed?"

I looked glum and felt like a puppy somebody kicked. I didn't want to voice my fears and give them power, but I needed a confidant. I grew up so secluded and sheltered, my brief foray at college notwithstanding. I just didn't have the experience with men to know if I was overreacting or correct in my criticisms.

"I think he regrets telling me his feelings, Andrea. I think he wants to break up with me before we've even gone on a date or had our third kiss. Maybe he wanted a bit of light-hearted fun. It's not like I flat-out demanded marriage of him, even though it's been on my mind. But that's just it. Don't you see? When I get flummoxed, it's easy for other witches to read my thoughts. What if Lorcan read mine, realized I was picturing white gowns and flowers, and now he's planning to buy a one-way ticket to Outer Mongolia?"

Andrea threw her head back and howled out a laugh, much to my chagrin, then immediately sobered when she saw the hurt cross my face.

"No! Oh, Lily...no, you misunderstand. I am not laughing at you. You are all over the place lately. You spent most of the holiday season worrying about nefarious evildoers out to destroy you and our family. Only it was a bit of fun concocted by our great-grandpa and Keisha Holcomb. And now you imagine the worst in a relationship that is just budding into something new and wonderful. You are supposed to be enjoying this moment, not freaking out over every little thing! Oh, honey, you're a hot mess."

"I am a hot mess. I'm a cold one too...lukewarm even."

Maybe Andrea was correct, and I am channeling my mom —um—aunt, Jessica, the conspiracy theorist par excellence, and worrying at shadows. There had to be an explanation for why Lorcan has suddenly gone off me. Although, if I was honest here, he seemed perfectly fine. There was no tension or awkwardness. Nothing had changed between us, and I expect that's what rankled. What did I expect him to do? Profess his undying love, sweep me off my feet and make passionate love to me in front of the entire town so they'd recognize our status? And just what was our situation? After all, I asked Lorcan if he'd help me get through the drama and heartache involving my parents, and he promised me he'd be there until the end of time. Could I have misunderstood his intent?

No. Not after that second kiss and his saying he's loved me since we were little, playing at games, yet realizing even then that we being together is our destiny. Not since professing he'd been searching for someone to erase the memory of me ever since I'd left, to no avail. Those weren't idle words to be tossed about and discarded later when they became inconvenient. No. Lorcan said he loved me. Now I just had to figure out what was bothering my big lug of a mechanic. Could it be this Tribunal thing Andrea mentioned?

I just had to add it to my long list of things I needed to accomplish before my world imploded with evil witches wanting to bring the war to our doorstep, rescue my father and free my mother from her furry prison, and save said prison in the process. Wicked had been subdued since my great-grandmother, Adriana, declared that she and Adelaide were one-and-the-same, or, rather, cohabiting in the same space.

Adriana!

"Oh, jeebers! Andrea! I forgot I am supposed to be meeting Granny at the library soon. If I hurry, I will just make it. I didn't drive to work today, so I need to leave now. Will you be OK with me running out on you?"

"Go...go. Granny will be in a sour mood if you are even ten seconds late for your meeting. Why the library anyway?" Andrea asked as she gathered up our lunch stuff and tossed it in the trash can.

"Something about doing some research into dark magic. But I can't imagine Sweet Briar's library having anything like that on its shelves, witch town or no witch town!"

As I tore out of my warehouse and ran across the street, I lamented again my decision to leave my truck at home. In my rush to get to the library, I wasn't paying much attention to where I was heading and almost got smushed by a passing pickup truck. I heard the brakes squeal in protest at having to stop short before I noticed it approaching from the corner of my eye.

"Eek!" I flung myself toward the curb, my heart slamming in my chest.

"What in the heck is wrong with you...running out in the street like that? Are you daft, woman? You're lucky I always drive a few ticks under the legal speed limit, or I'd have flattened you under my tires about now! I never drive over the limit, and it's because of loony jaywalkers and daydreamers like you!" Harley Jacobs, a dairy farmer in town and one-time sweetheart of the dearly departed Deanna Fredericks, groused at me through his window as I clutched my chest.

"Mister Jacobs. I'm so sorry. I am late to meet my great-grandmother at the library and wasn't thinking straight or paying attention."

"You're damn straight you ain't thinking. You're going to wind up getting yourself killed, young lady." Harley pulled over to the curb, hopped out of his truck, slamming the door, and stomped over to me, slapping his ball cap on his knee. "You need to be more aware of what's going on around you. Although this might be a fortuitous meeting."

Harley lowered his voice after glancing around and leaned toward me, "I need to talk private-like with you. I found some old items and know some things about Deanna and Donna, and I can't keep my mouth shut no more. When can I come around and speak to you? And mebbe your granny?"

"Oh, well... I'm not sure? Can you give me your number, and I will call you after I meet with her today? Can't you just tell me what it is now?"

"Not now...not here." Harley looked around as if he suspected to be overheard and couldn't risk it. "Here. This here's my business card for the farm. Call me when you get with your granny and can meet up with me. Try to be quick about it. I need to tell you some things."

And with that, Harley Jacobs tipped his cap and shuffled back into his truck and drove off.

Noting the time, I groaned. Now I definitely would not be on time to meet Adriana.

CHAPTER 2

"*Y*ou're late."

"I am not."

"You are."

"I'm not!"

"Yes, you are. What's with the paperclip in your hair?"

"No, I am not...late is anything after ten minutes. It's barely two past the hour." I reached up, found the paperclip, and removed it, but not before yanking out several strands of my long black hair, and tossed the offending clip onto the table. Granny peered down at it with a frown and whisked it away.

"You are too. Martha, tell my great-granddaughter that she has kept me waiting for nearly three whole minutes, and yet she insists she isn't late."

"Uh..." My friend Martha looked back and forth between us, then spun quickly and rushed to answer the telephone at the main desk. It wasn't even ringing.

"Coward." Adriana cackled at her retreating back.

"Can you blame her? You are snippy and argumentative.

She probably doesn't want to get into the middle of a witch fight."

"Heh. Witch fight. And I am not argumentative. You. Are. Late."

My great-grandmother emphasized this point by tapping her index finger on the table with each utterance.

"I almost got flattened by Harley Jacobs while heading this way. He wants to talk to both of us, something about Donna and Deanna. So that is why I am a bit behind, but hardly late. And I'm sorry, but didn't you make me wait a full twenty minutes, tummy rumbling when you failed to meet me at Joe's at our designated time last week?"

"Hey! I'm old and feeble. It takes me a long time to walk around town."

"Feeble my asparagus! First of all, you drove. Second, you only claim you are feeble when trying to get out of trouble or seeking sympathy. And third, just yesterday, I saw you chase Maureen Kennedy up Main Street until you tackled her to the ground and made her cry. What was up with that anyway?"

Adriana Dolce, pushing if not already over one hundred —I still hadn't asked, could probably outrun any professional football player, and her tackling prowess would be the envy of any linebacker in the NFL.

"She sassed me, so I made her eat dirt."

"Don't you think that was a bit extreme?" I asked, even though I was secretly pleased Granny had taken on the conceited teenager who worked for my friend, June Carter, at her shop, June's Emporium. Maureen and I hadn't gotten off on the right foot. We hadn't gotten off on the left one either. She was a bully, and she hadn't outgrown her imma-ture shenanigans since leaving her school days behind. Many older teens and young adults in town still quaked when her shadow crossed their path.

Maureen took an instant dislike to me, probably because I didn't put up with her attitude and wasn't impressed with her reputation. Mean girls didn't scare me. Let's face it, and a bully is just an insecure weakling asking for attention. She was able to trick the adults into thinking she was a pleasant and darling thing. Of course, now that she's pushing twenty and carrying an extra twenty, she isn't so cute anymore. June never bought her act...so why she kept her on was a mystery.

Adriana just smiled at the memory and shrugged.

"Not really. I have to stop by Harley's farm in a couple of days. He can wait until then. Don't try to use that as an excuse for being late."

"Anyway, I am here now... what's this meeting about?" I asked, barely suppressing an eye roll.

"Research. We need to hit the books, find that spell and learn how to reverse it. This way, we can deal with Adelaide and that cat of yours and free them from being bound together. I suspect we can find traces of who borrowed it from the library. I also need to look up lore on sweet briar rose magic and discover why Wicked protects the bush growing outside your back door. Or is it Adelaide that's protecting it? I don't know who is in control there, another reason for the research."

I regarded my great-grandmother skeptically and snorted.

"I hate to inform you of this, but I doubt the Sweet Briar Library is going to have books to give us that answer, witch town or no witch town," I said this in hushed tones, not sure if the patrons wandering around were all our kind.

The town had a spell cast over it where tourists and regular non-magical people wouldn't be able to hear us when we spoke of anything witchy. They misheard what we were saying or had a suggestion implanted that would make them not try to listen in. It seemed foolproof, yet I still got the willies whenever I happened to be in public and made statements involving magic and spellcasting—today was no exception.

"That's what you think, Miss Smarty Pants. It shows what you know. Andiamo!"

"Hurry up? Where are we going?"

"To the prohibited section."

"Oh, no, you don't! I forbid it!"

No sooner had Granny uttered those words, Edith Plank, former head librarian and current spook about town, popped in to demand we cease and desist. How she knew we were here and why she even cared anymore; I didn't know. Let's face it. She's a ghost. One that only Adriana and I seemed to be able to see. Well, except for a few others like Chester and Hester Soule, the town's resident undertakers. But they didn't count, seeing as it was part and parcel of what they did —the creepy freaks.

"Edith! Go away. You need to stop following me around. Go haunt your family."

Edith ignored me and whooshed over to Adriana, who was marching purposefully toward the back hall that led to the employee area, comprised of the break room, restroom, and back exit.

"You can't do this, Adriana. I forbid it. That is a highly classified area, and even my family wasn't allowed down there when I was in charge. Only the Elders can enter, and that's with a vote and full meetings on the subject. Those are the rules! You are no longer an Elder. You have to have good reason to go down there, and..."

"And when have you ever known me to listen to the rules, Edie?" And with that, Adrianna waltzed into the ladies' room and entered a stall. I stood on the other side, scratching my head and glaring at... Edie?

"Edie? Really? You let her call you that?"

"Oh, stuff it, Lily. She can't get away with this. Dolce or no Dolce. You have to stop her!" Edith whined.

"I'm going to have to wait until she's, um, finished in there." Like no way was I going to follow my Granny into the stall and confront her while taking care of business.

"You moron! That's the entrance. Hurry up and follow her before she causes the alarms to go off!"

Alarms? I tentatively opened the stall door and found a nondescript toilet staring back at me. Where did Adriana go? I looked dubiously at the bowl and hoped I wouldn't have to enter it like some Harry Potter flushing spell thingy. There was no way in heck I'd go that route.

"Close the stall door. Come on, Lily. You are running out of time."

"OK, then what? Edith? Hello?" When she didn't respond, I rolled my eyes, opened the door again and found myself in The Chamber of Secrets. Seriously. I know I said no to any Harry Potter movie stuff, but I was now in an almost exact replica of what I remembered the space under Hogwarts to look like from my movie-watching experience.

Extra-large moss-covered stone block walls with tall columns embedded in them every twenty feet or so with intricate mythical animal shapes on the walls looking like snakes, wyrms, and dragons. Sconces lined the walls on either side that appeared to be iron with actual flames flickering in them to light the way. There was only one path to take, and that was forward.

"Whoa."

I glanced back at the stall door only to realize from this side it seemed like something you'd find in a dungeon. All heavy wood and forged ornamental iron strap hinges, spearhead handles and sporting a door knocker looking like a dragon's head. OK, then. I wondered what would happen if I went back in the way I had come, but I didn't want to leave my great-grandmother behind, even though I was sure she'd be just fine.

And where did Edith go? One minute she was jumping up and down, shouting I hurry and corral Adriana and stop her from doing whatever she was about to do; the next instant, she is gone, and I am in an alternate universe of holy terror. All I needed was spiderwebs with their creepy-crawly residents on them to send me shrieking back to the safety of the library. Although for all its outward, antediluvian appearances, the place seemed spotless.

Turning back around, I cautiously proceeded to follow the expansive hallway, my footfalls muffled on an ornate jeweled-toned rug, to the opposite end, and was relieved to find my great-grandmother standing before another impressive door. This one had a frowning demon's head or some such embedded into it. The face wore a horrid countenance, with bared teeth and a lolling tongue, not another door-knocker like the one behind us, but more of a sentry—guarding the way. I didn't like this one bit and said so.

"Don't be silly. There is no reason for you to worry. We've sealed this place off for a very long time. And what Edith doesn't know is even with a vote, no one would have been able to open this door until now."

"Why is that?" I asked, noticing there didn't seem to be a knob or handle of any kind, and I couldn't see how we were supposed to open it even if Granny knew.

"Because Charlie sealed it twenty-one years ago before he left, and only his blood can open it."

"Well, I hate to tell you this, but we don't have his blood on us, so you dragged me here for nothing."

Adriana glanced over at me and smiled evilly. Then she pulled a small dagger out of her pocket and grabbed my hand.

"No, but we have yours. Hold tight."

And with that, my demented tormentor slashed the blade across my hand, cutting me deep enough so that blood spurt out. I shrieked and went to pull away, but Adriana, with the formidable strength I've mentioned, raised my hand and ran it across the demon's protruding tongue. Only then did she release my wrist.

"You witch! You are evil, nasty... I can't believe you did that to me! I'm bleeding and in pain! Why would... hey!"

I looked down as Adriana waved her hand in my direction. A bluish-purple sparkling strand of magic flowed out from her fingertips and encircled my palm, which instantly stopped hurting. When I glanced down, there wasn't even a mark where the blade had cut. Just as the last remnants of pain faded, the telltale sound of the ancient door's hinges creaked in protest as it shuddered. It echoed down the hall and reverberated back to us with a deep grumble.

"Even so, old woman. Why didn't you do that to yourself and leave me out of it?" I'd protested, rubbing the spot where the cut had been.

"Because my Charlie was smart. He understood this area was dangerous. Vile even. And he knew once he disappeared going after you, Jessica, and Addy, I would have been down here in a flash and broken every rule to find him. So, he made the reverse spell go down a generation, not up to Chiara or me nor Antonio. If Charles wasn't here to open the door with his blood, you could only do it with yours. I figured that out when he made you director of the library in the papers he'd left behind. Why do you think Edith was so upset with you for trying to take her job?"

"But I wasn't trying to take her job. I didn't even know about this. You set me up!"

"Oh, pisht."

"Really? That's all you are going to say for yourself. Do

you honestly think I am going to let you get away with attacking me? I am going to tell..."

My voice trailed off into a tiny squeak when I noticed the devil face had gone from frowning to a self-satisfied leer, and I almost gagged when he lapped at the blood—my blood—then licked his lips clean.

"Hmmm...nice. I taste a sweet Dolce once more. Get it? Sweet? I recognize you, too, old witch. You know the rules, perhaps better than most. Heed my warning, though. Take anything from the rooms beyond, and my wrath will be horrible and swift. You may go forth."

My mouth was hanging open so low I was sure I looked like Daffy Duck in all those old cartoons, only I couldn't seem to reach up and close mine. Moths were hovering nearby, I'm sure, waiting to take up residence in my gaping maw. It was only until Adriana grabbed my wrist and pulled me forward that I snapped it shut and meekly allowed her to drag me past the ogling imp, who gave me a disgusting once-over as I passed. Like... *ew.*

We entered a similar but much narrower corridor and started walking. The flames in the sconces lining the walls dimmed, making it difficult to see very far ahead. As we wandered along a thick red carpet, the sound of our footfall muffled. I wasn't scared, per se, more nerves mixed with curiosity, but I was still smarting over being used as a sacrificial lamb by Adriana.

She didn't make conversation as we went along, and I started to wonder as the hallway became a trek of epic proportions without any end in sight.

"Just how long is this hall anyway? How far do we have to go?" I whined.

"About three miles end to end," Adriana stated primly and kept her brisk pace.

I stopped short.

"Three miles? Do we have to walk three miles? Where the heck is this place leading us? Three miles is... it's... it's three miles!"

"If I can do it, you can as well." Adriana chided.

What happened with old and feeble? Her sprightliness just proved my point that she only complains and uses that excuse to get sympathy or get out of whatever trouble she's managed to find herself.

Sighing, I hurried to catch up and kept marching forward, but after a bit, my side started to twinge, and I was thirsty. I reached in my pockets and pulled out a few black jellybeans I always had on me. They would have to do.

I noticed a shift in temperature as if we went from a dank dungeon to slightly more temperate conditions. Suddenly I spied another door in the distance. This one had another two demon faces on them, but these two seemed to be little orna-mentation, nothing else. They were embedded in the doors, padded in a rich green satin-type fabric with button indenta-tions, swinging doors of some type that you'd see in a luxu-rious art deco restaurant from the twenties or thirties, one that would separate the kitchen from the dining areas.

Only these didn't contain those small windows one would peak through before coming out holding a tray piled high with food. I didn't think I'd need to shed any more blood to pass through them, but I still tucked my hands behind my back and slowed down, letting Adriana enter first. No way was I going to be the first in line for whatever was waiting on the other side.

I didn't know what I was expecting after the medieval hallway, but nothing could prepare me for what I faced on the other side of the demon doors.

Nothing.

CHAPTER 3

*M*y mind had conjured some ideas on what I'd find beyond the corridor. A massive library with floor-to-ceiling shelving and giant iron ladders on wheels to reach the upper tomes? A dusty and dank dungeon with medieval monks who had long since expired, yet scribbled still in an unholy and unearthly way; eyes vacant but quills rushing across the pages, ink blotters at the ready? A roomful of goblins with long pointy teeth waiting to bite my hand off should I dare touch anything forbidden?

Yeah, see? All of that would have seemed normal... almost. Instead, I followed Adriana into a room eerily reminiscent of how they depicted heaven in Monty Python's, The Meaning of Life. If you've not seen it yet, get thee to a movie channel posthaste.

No, Death didn't escort us into a schmaltzy room with diners and music, waiters running hither and yon. It was more like a pseudo-library with opulent overtones eerily similar to the movie's banquet room, however.

Instead of a smattering of round tables strewn about, there was an abundance of sage-green velvet-lined chairs arranged in a way that one could easily converse with one's neighbor. Matching drapery lined the walls, from floor to the lofty heights of the ceiling above, green—instead of the rosy, pink ones in the aforementioned movie, that matched the chairs.

However, the floor was cloud-like with billowing smoke making it difficult to see where we were walking or what we walked on. There was even a long white staircase that led up to a platform of sorts, and that's where I finally saw my first sign of life in the shape of an exceedingly tiny man dressed in a long, flowing, white robe, a circlet of gold laurel leaves resting on his balding head. He was sporting bejeweled cat-eye spectacles complete with a long chain around his neck to keep them from falling off his head.

He glanced up when he heard us approach, and his face broke into a wide, welcoming grin as he trotted down to meet us, with arms outstretched toward Adriana.

"Annie! My dear. What an extreme pleasure this is. I haven't seen you in what? Forty or so odd years now? How are you, darling?" He had a slight lisp and an effeminate manner that made me suspect he might bat for the same team if you know what I mean. Not that there was anything wrong with this, but I certainly hadn't expected to find a gay, dwarf-like man in a toga, and wait... he had on heels!

Noticing my shock upon spying his footwear, the little man beamed at me, nodding in the affirmative as he explained, "I do so love how these give me stature. The Good Lord didn't bless me with height, honey, but these shoes make me feel like a rock star!"

Yeah, Elton John's less garish tiny brother, if I had to guess.

"I can offer tea, cookies, and a little gossip. And let me tell you, it has been slim pickings lately, what with dear Edith going off on her grand afterlife adventure keeping me from hearing all the juicy tidbits circulating town. She used to text me all the gossip from up above. You need to tell her replacement, Martha; I think that's her name. It would help if you told her to send down more minutiae and not forget I'm still guarding this place. A girl gets bored down here alone!"

Text? Girl?

He did look a bit like Nathan Lane from The Birdcage, although he desperately needed a shave—and not just his face! So, I let the 'girl' comment go and smiled brightly at the friendly dwarf.

"And whom do we have here?" Reaching out to take my hand, the tiny man spun me around in a pirouette while taking in my appearance, nodding in approval at what he saw. "Oh! Hang on a minute! This isn't? But it can't be! Oh ho! So, the prodigal daughter has returned after all. I'd wondered when I began hearing whispers from above. It seems the rumors are true! Same dark hair, same cognac brown eyes, the longest lashes any girl has the right to be flashing—and natural to boot! But I detect a bit of Croy mixed in with the Dolce. Charlie Sweet's baby girl has returned to Sweet Briar. Welcome, sweet Liliana. Or do you go by Lily?"

"I, uh... I'm sorry but do I know you? Have we met?" I asked forehead wrinkled in confusion at his familiarity with me.

"Have we met? Have we met! Oh, honey, I changed your diaper. I rocked you more times than I can remember. I sprinkled pixie dust over your eyes to make you drowsy. I sang show tunes in a whisper until you giggled yourself to sleep! I'm your fairy-godfather, of course, we've met."

Why did this proclamation not surprise me in the slightest?

* * *

"I NEED to get in there, Jerry."

"Not gonna happen, doll. I'm sorry."

"Jerry...you owe me, and you know it." This from Adriana, who had been working the dwarf over for the last thirty minutes to no avail.

And Jerry? Really?

"That is neither here nor there. I can't help you break the law. I won't do it. You know better than to try to get me to concede. Do you think you can get past me? Or worse, convince me to break the laws for you? Do I look like a fool?"

Hold that thought.

I had wandered over to one of the comfy chairs and plopped myself down to wait out this mild battle of wills happening before me. My bet was on the tiny dude. Fairy-godfather! Leave it to me to have a fairy-godfather—a gay one. Which, in hindsight, might be a good thing considering those shoes he was wearing were Louboutin's, and maybe he'd pass on some much-needed fashion sense to me. Or man advice.

I went from surreal to insane weeks ago. I was almost sad I didn't have more of a reaction to all of this madness and just shrugged it off. However, the easy-listening music piping in on unseen speakers was giving me the heebie-jeebies. I even jolted when Barry Manilow started singing about leaving behind a lost love during a weekend in New England, the moment bittersweet.

"I just love me some Barry... don't you agree, Lily?"

"Um..."

Anything I was going to say was drowned out by a deep grinding sound reverberating throughout the room, although it seemed to be coming from the top of the stairs. Jerry appeared shocked at the sound, then gave Adriana a hurt glare before squinting at her in disappointment.

"You did not! Tell me you didn't go behind my back,

usurping my authority and called The Keeper of Tomes. Go ahead. Tell me."

"Jerry, you whine entirely too much. I simply stated my case, and The Keeper is reasonable enough to know some laws are meant to be broken or bent as it were." Adriana patted the minuscule man on the head and swept around him, heading for the stairs. She flicked her wrist at me, demanding I join her at the bottom step.

"I don't understand. Who is The Keeper of Tomes? Why do you need permission, and if you could make a phone call and get in here, why on earth did we have to walk three flipping miles?" I still wasn't over that jaunt, probably because Adriana was barely winded at the end of it while I was breathing heavily from the effort.

"Because you can only enter the chamber where they keep the books when the Keeper of Tomes opens the ward on one side, and someone else—someone with permission—who has travailed the path and left a sacrifice to the guardian at the first door, opens it from the other. Jerry, here, is a distraction to flummox anyone who thinks they've broken through the barrier. He'd hit them with one banality after another, lame music playing softly, and all the while, the Sentinels would be tracking their every movement waiting to strike."

Wait. Sentinels? I wouldn't say I liked the sound of that.

"But we are cleared, right? I mean, you said you spoke with The Keeper, so we're allowed in, no?"

My great-grandmother just smiled enigmatically and said, "Come along cara." Just as a loud gong began to sound in the distance, we started our ascent, leaving Jerry grumbling behind in our wake.

I felt my anticipation growing with every step we climbed as my hands began to sweat. My nerves were going haywire as my heart rate began to accelerate. Who or what could possibly be waiting for us on the other side of this next door? My imagination was in overdrive, and I had the sudden urge to hightail it in the opposite direction, even if it meant running three miles back to the safety of the toilet stall. But hang on now! I was a dark witch. I could handle whatever was beyond... right?

I peered back at Jerry when we reached the top of the landing, but he'd disappeared. Where could he have gone so quickly? I glanced every which way but couldn't spy him anywhere unless he went through the way we had entered, although that didn't seem feasible. That's when I noted the music had stopped playing as well, and the lights began to dim as if we were in a movie theater.

The door in front of us opened slowly, and I gulped. Then we entered and found... Susanne Washington?

CHAPTER 4

*A*re you kidding me? All this drama and mystery, not to mention nerve-wracking tension, and I walk into a smallish dusty room with books and parchment lying everywhere, and our friend Susanne Washington is this Keeper person?

"You've got to be joking! Susanne! You are a Methodist church lady who sings in the choir." And I could hear faint *hallelujahs* and *praise the Lord's* drifting down from up above, so I suspect we are under the African Methodist Church a few miles out of town heading north from the square, "there is no way you are The Keeper of Tomes! You aren't even a witch, wait, are you?"

Shoulders rocking gently with mirth, Susanne came over to me and hugged me, patting my back, then did the same to Adriana before walking over to a central square table where she sat. She pulled a lilac-colored sweater around her shoulders to ward off the chill in the air, tucking a handkerchief into her sleeve as she did. Her face broke into a dimpled smile as she motioned us to do the same before responding.

"My daddy and his daddy before him were the original

Keepers for Sweet Briar and his momma before that. I am indeed a witch, just not a very powerful one. Although having the key to this chamber in my possession does come with a certain amount of hubris, I think."

Well, alrighty then. I sat across from Susanne and noticed a large book on the table, which seemed to quiver in anticipation as we drew near. I could almost hear whispered thoughts and soft words seemingly coming from the pages in a jumble of unintelligible prose. Now that I think about it, all the books in the room seemed to be whispering.

Avoiding the obvious white elephant on the table before me, I turned to Susanne and made small talk for the time being.

"Do you still occasionally work for the loathsome Reverend Brewster and his rigid wife, Laura?" The Brewster's had a small congregation on the outskirts of our town. I'd recently learned he lost his position as rector in another larger church, denomination unknown, which is why he decided to branch out on his own. He formed the *Everlasting Love of The Lord Upon High Holy Redeemer Evangelical Church.* Yeah. Trying to say that five times fast.

The place appeared more like an old doctor's office, abandoned, however, complete with peeling pink shutters and flamingos—also pink—in abundance on the weed-infested lawn—not that flamingos were requisite to doctor's offices. Susanne cleaned for them every so often—or used to—as did the evil Donna Fredericks before starting her quest to take down my small family.

Andrea and I had a run-in with the lecherous Reverend Oliver and his wife, Laura, she of the squinty eyes and judgmental demeanor. Laura took one look at the thin streaks of rich purple I had dyed parts of my hair and instantly thought devil worshiper or fornicator, or whatever slur to my name she could think up. Like a few purple streaks meant I was an evildoer.

They had been part of my very first investigation when I'd arrived in Sweet Briar, not that it was much of anything since the two women who saved the day and my bacon, were the very two women sitting with me now. Adriana and Susanne had barreled in, magic twitching and guns blazing, and subdued evil Donna until Brian Chase, detective, and my ex-boyfriend, could come in and arrest her.

"Life is too short to surround yourself with such folks: sour dispositions and unyielding ideals. I do believe those two need to loosen their shorts a touch. No. I no longer give them my precious time." Susanne smiled then gazed pointedly down at the tome, forcing me to address its presence—open and waiting on the table.

"It's your show." I stated, turning to my great-grandmother and pointing to the book, "what's next?"

"Touch the book, Liliana."

I wouldn't say I liked the sound of that. *At all.* Like, I began scooting my butt backward in the chair while shaking my head no.

"You touch it. I've already had my hand lacerated." Turning toward Susanne, I gave her my most hangdog expression and continued, "My great-grandmother sliced me open and slathered my blood on the door back there, then made me walk three miles. I am still traumatized about this, and now she wants me to touch a whispering book? No way. It probably bites."

Susanne gave me a sympathetic smile and reached her hand out to me before saying, "Lily. Please, touch the book."

Et Tu, Susie?

Sighing, I cautiously reached my hand out, fully expecting the tome to jump up and attack. Placing my hand down on the pages, I felt a trembling sensation, not unlike a cat purring. Then it settled to a gradual humming vibration, ever so soft and not threatening in the slightest.

"Sit back now, dear." Susanne leaned forward along with Adriana while I acquiesced and sat back once more.

We waited.

Nothing.

I was about to suggest I try touching it again when the pages began turning on their own in a blur of movement. When the pages settled once more, I found myself edging close again, curiosity getting the better of me. I was about to mention the words seemed like chicken scratch, but then I noticed a glance pass between Adriana and Susanne and felt butterflies begin dancing around my stomach.

"What? What does it mean? Ladies, please don't keep me in suspense here. I saw the look that passed between you."

"This is a directory of sorts. And it seems that whatever tome we need is on the lowest level, and you must retrieve it." Adriana professed, turning to Susanne for confirmation.

"That about sums it up. I'm sorry, dear."

"OK...hold on. Why are you sorry?"

Adriana looked distinctly uncomfortable, and the butterflies turned into a swarm. I already knew I would not be pleased with her response. "Because you are going to have to go through the Sentinels to get it."

I'm ashamed to say I blew up and started shouting at the two older women. Clearly, they expected this and didn't seem too disturbed that I was frothing at the mouth and storming around the room like a psychopath. I would have to be insane to listen to the dire duo, and their doom is awaiting me Sentinel proclamation. At this point, I could probably storm the prison where they were holding Donna Fredricks and strangle the information we needed out of her.

Hang on. That wasn't such a bad idea!

"Why are we doing all this...this...*lunacy,* when we can

sneak in where they're holding Donna and beat her into submission? I don't even know what Sentinels *are*, but I sure as heck think a few prison guards will be a whole lot better to confront."

Adriana gave me a weighted look, "I've already been to see Donna Fredricks."

I blinked, dumbfounded.

"You have? But, well, what did she have to say for herself? Did you need to put the thumbscrews to her until she squealed? Why didn't you tell me in the first place? All this time and we could have avoided bloodshed—my bloodshed—and that long walk. What did you find out from that woman?"

"I didn't find anything out."

OK, I'd had enough of these cryptic responses.

"Why not?"

"Because she wasn't where she was supposed to be. The Council misplaced her."

My mouth was hanging open again, and it stayed that way for a good count of twenty before I began to laugh. My mouth was still hanging open, so I am sure I looked like a hysterical maniac. And don't get me started on that word. I hate it, its etymology, and everything it stands for, but right now, I could honestly say I was going to go into a fit of hysterics.

"How can the Council lose a person? Is she... no. No more questions. Explain."

I sat back down, crossing my arms across my chest. The only sign I was a hair-trigger away from exploding again was my leg moving back and forth in agitation.

"What do you want me to say? They thought they put her in one section, but when they searched, she wasn't there. It's not like she can escape from the wards, so she is in there, somewhere. Just where, exactly, is still a mystery."

How do you like that? My confidence in the ability of the Council to handle essential matters just decreased tenfold. This prison was supposed to be tighter than Alcatraz, run with military-like precision. Instead, we seemed to be stuck with the Keystone Cops.

"What are they currently doing about it?"

"They have their own set of Sentinels that are hunting her. Mark my words, if she is hiding in a cave, crack, or crevice, the Sentinels, will find her. I just hope they don't squish her like a bug when they do."

"Squish?"

"Like a bug."

And they wanted me to go down a few levels into that cave of hell and outrun another set of Sentinels?

"Just what are these guardians like anyway? I mean, are we talking Cyclops or what?"

"Worse."

We sat in silence, and I could hear the faint voices from the choir above us as they finished another round of hymns, scraping and sliding noises telling me they were done for the day and heading home.

"And when am I to face these leviathans of the deep anyway? Right now?"

"No. We will come back when you are more prepared. I hadn't anticipated this outcome. We need to have a family meeting and plan our next move. Your next move. Basically, we need to brainstorm."

There was no brain in any of what I was about to do; calling it brainstorming was a lesson in futility.

CHAPTER 5

T'd like to say Adriana called the family meeting first thing the next day. It didn't happen. She had spent an hour pouring over books in that small room, finding some hints here and there but no real answers. Those, she insisted, would be in the forbidden area and more than likely a passage or two out of an ancient tome which held the darkest of magic.

My patience was growing thin because all I had on my mind was freeing Adelaide and saving Wicked, finding the elusive Donna and beating information out of her before the Elders locked her in solitary—and hoped this time she'd stay put. I also wanted to release the siren song spell at full strength, hoping it would be the enticing beacon we needed it to be to draw my father home—or lead us to him. All these delays were making me one frustrated witch.

Instead, trying to get everyone together at the same time had us waiting until Sunday when everyone freed up, and the consensus was to convene at my home. I was OK with this because the workers I'd hired completed most of the renovations, and I was itching to host a dinner in my big, homey dining room. I decided a big bowl of spaghetti would do because I wasn't confident with my cooking skills just yet, but spaghetti I could handle.

I still had to clean up some contractor dust and needed to tackle wallpaper, the floors needed buffing, and there was plenty of indoor painting to be finished, but it was functional now that I had brand new kitchen appliances. I decided it might be time to head up to the attic and go through the boxes purported to hold my parent's possessions—more specifically, plates, dishes, cups, and spoons...anything to get me to stop using plastic. Especially since it would make my Adriana's left eye twitch when she'd drop in, and the one lone spoon I owned was dirty in the sink, forcing her to use the plastic stuff.

As it was only Saturday, I decided to put in a few hours of work in my studio and get some online orders ready to be shipped the following week. I didn't get much foot traffic during the week when I was open and did much of my art on consignment. That would change when the festival season ratcheted up again, and tourists would descend upon us. I had much of my art sprinkled around town at various shops that carried local artisans' works, and I planned on getting a tented booth at the fairgrounds once they were completed this spring.

One block off the village square, the middle school, had built a new sports field and playground complex that connected them with the neighboring high school to the north, so the previous field had sat forlorn and empty. That is until the Winters Sisters, Hermione, and Hortense—two new witchy residents to our town—suggested it be turned into a festival area to expand on our artsy folk village theme. Since it is walking distance to the square, being one street over, and had ample room for parking, the business leaders and town council thought it a grand idea, and work was going fast and furious since early January. Now, barely into February, we were starting to see some real progress.

The fairgrounds would be a year-round open-end market with paved parking, artisan and craft booths on one end, a central indoor-outdoor market, and concessions with a few more specialty booths on the other end. There was even talk of turning the old administration building and gymnasium, which was moving to the high school grounds, into an auction house. This way not only would local farmers and artists and those in witchy crafting professions be prominent selling their wares, but the town could have a permanent structure that catered to gently used and precious antiques. Having an indoor event center would be a huge draw and income generator as well. Right now, the construction crews were busy adding brick pathways, a central fountain, and charming streetlamps that appeared as if they were burning gas but were artificial with bulbs that flickered.

I, for one, couldn't wait.

"There you are. You ran out of here on Thursday to go meet your granny, and I haven't seen you around since." Lorcan wandered into my warehouse from the alley that joined his mechanic shop to mine. He carried a to-go cup tray of java from Enchanté Café, my Uncle Stephen, and Aunt Chiara's place. My interest piqued when I noticed a paper bag dangling below it—hoping it contained one of my uncle's incredible offerings. That hope turned to reality when Lorcan set the coffee down on my workstation and handed me the bag. I opened it to find two perfect cannoli inside just waiting for me.

"You didn't get anything for yourself?"

Lorcan looked mildly concerned then gave me a lopsided grin when he recognized I was teasing. He *thought* I was teasing. I was not.

"You're welcome to mine, you know."

"You should never offer me your cannoli and hope I won't take you up on it...but because you have no clue the depths of my devotion to them, I will spare you...this time."

Lorcan glanced back toward his place, then came up and gave me a hug followed by a soft kiss. I tried to remain aloof, but it was a losing battle. I just loved being in his arms way too much, and he knew it. Lorcan had a smile on his face when our lips parted, but as my face fell and he noticed my misery, concern replaced his smile. He tucked a lock of my hair behind my ear, tilting my chin up so our eyes met again.

"I know why you're upset, and I'm sorry we haven't had a chance to talk. Listen, it's Saturday. I don't have to be here today. The good mayor is here, working on some cars he didn't get to this week. Jack is supposed to come in for an hour or two later on, and you aren't really open either. Why don't we wrap up this stuff and head over to your place? Or we can go to mine."

The 'good mayor' was Stu Jones, Lorcan's part-time mechanic and, much to my utter surprise, the town leader. If you knew Stu, you too would be shocked with this information. Let's just say he isn't the brightest bulb in the socket, the quickest horse in the race, or the fastest talker in the auction house. There were times he'd pause between replying to something you'd asked him, that you were sure he fell asleep standing up with his eyes open. But if you gave it a minute—or ten, he usually started up again.

I considered what Lorcan suggested and liked it enough that I began tossing supplies in their respective places. Knowing he lived in a renovated apartment above his parent's garage paying them rent, I figured we'd have more privacy at my place and said so even though his family home was just an open garden gate stroll from mine. He agreed, giving me another quick peck on the cheek, then went back to his side to inform Stu he finished for the day.

Since I'd walked the few blocks to work this morning, Lorcan offered to drive me home. That's how I wound up on the front bench of his Chevy pickup when Edith Plank decided to pop in between us, a smug grin on her ghostly face.

"Gah!"

"What? What's wrong?" Lorcan had hit the brakes so hard; my chest hurt from the seat belt.

"Edith! Get out of this truck. Now. What are you doing here?"

Lorcan sighed, rolling his eyes, and pulled into the street, heading south around the square, then turned right back on Main Street before making the second left onto Wildflower Lane, my street. My friends and family had gotten used to Edith haunting me from time to time, usually on a whim, although she had tried saving me from a murderous construction worker recently. So I tried to be tolerant.

"Do you know how boring my family is? I've spent the last three weeks wandering around the manor, and all daddy does is read, and momma sits there and drinks, even if it's before noon. Grandmama and Pop, Pop is no better. Why won't you tell them I'm fine—happy even, and let them have some bit of joy and closure?"

I didn't have the heart to tell her I suspected the Langsford and Dietrich clans would be that dour and gloomy even if Edith were still among the living.

"Edith, I honestly do not think your family would appreciate me showing up with a story that you are a spook, and I am the only one who can see or hear you. Well, except for Granny and a few other folks. Why don't you go ask the Soule's to pay a visit? I'm sure they'd love to drum up future business while on a compassionate mission such as yours!"

Edith sulked lips in a pout.

"Is she pouting?" Lorcan asked.

I nodded yes and sighed.

Edith had a sly look cross her face and cuddled up to Lorcan.

"Isn't he such a darling man? So cute. I bet he's a good kisser, am I right?" Then to my utter amazement, she stuck her tongue in his ear. Not that Lorcan could tell, but I did notice him shiver a bit as if he'd caught a chill.

"Get your tongue out of my boyfriend's ear!"

Lorcan jumped in his seat and began batting at his head, making shooing motions, then stuck his pinky in his ear, wiggling it about. He couldn't tell his hand just chopped through Edith's head, but it did make her back away, although she was laughing.

"Tell me it's gone. Her tongue! Tell me it's gone!"

"Lorcan, slow down! Turn. You're going to miss my drive."

Looking sheepish, Lorcan pulled into my driveway, and we tumbled out of the truck and walked to the back door hoping Edith would stay behind. The sweet briar rose bush that Wicked...um...Adelaide keeps protecting, stood forlorn in the February air, still chilly today. But a subtle shift had me thinking spring would come early to the south, unlike the Catskill Mountains, where I had lived for years before returning home.

Donald Murphy had shown up early this morning, as a matter of fact, and handed over last year's peas gone to seed, informing me I only had about one week to till my tiny vegetable patch and get them planted. I didn't know I had a vegetable patch to plant, let alone how to cultivate. Donald was so earnest though I figured a trip to the Ace Hardware in Clayton was in order since Dennis Carter didn't carry any at his store. Donald and his wife Doreen had put me up in their small country motel on my first night in Sweet Briar, and they remained close.

The minute I opened the door, I could see something

terrible had happened and rushed in through my mudroom into my cozy kitchen. Well, ordinarily cozy, but right now, it seemed like someone dumped cat food, my pea seeds, and even a wee potted variegated ivy plant I had purchased onto my beautiful heart of pine floor. Lorcan and I scrutinized the entire area, and our eyes landed on Wicked at precisely the exact moment. No further wondering was necessary. She still had dirt on her paws, and a self-satisfied cat look on her tiny hirsute face.

"You evil snot. Don't you dare give me that face, and don't try and blame Adelaide. This is one-hundred-percent pure feline hijinks. Why did you...oh." Belatedly, I realized that I had forgotten to feed my inky black hellcat in my rush to get those packages ready to ship for the upcoming week. "I'm sorry, OK? I mean... it's not like you'd starve or anything, and you have plenty of water."

Wicked gave me a disdainful scowl, jumped down from her perch, and trotted over to Lorcan. She looked up and gave him such a plaintive "Mreoo?" that we both glanced down to where her water bowl should have been sitting, filled and fresh, only to notice it was bone dry.

I am such an evil cat mommy.

"You suck at pet owner too? Half-assed dark witch and now animal cruelty? You should be ashamed of yourself."

"Edith! Go away. Go away now before I cook up a spell that will send you to Hades with a parka on!"

Edith laughed and wandered—OK, drifted—over to my den where she perched on the arm of my sofa. I think she did, anyway. When Edith sat, her derriere turned to smokey ectoplasm. It didn't stop her from giving me a glance with a mischievous gleam in her eyes. Ugh! *Ghosts!*

Turning back, I watched as Lorcan cleaned out and filled Wicked's bowl, then placed it back down near her feeding station. I went back around the counter and marched into the mudroom, where I grabbed the dustpan and broom, swept up the mess, and then brought it outside, dumping it over the porch railing. Sighing, I went back inside and righted my poor ivy plant, then gave it a bit of water to get over the shock of being flipped out of its pot. The pea seeds I had managed to pick up were now sitting in a small bowl.

With all of these tasks accomplished, I realized Lorcan, and I would have no privacy until I addressed Edith and found out why she was back yet again. There had to be a reason. There always was.

"Talk, Edith. What's up?"

Lorcan came over and went to sit down in one of the armchairs but paused, giving the room a once over, then tracked his eyes to me as if asking, is it safe to sit here or will I be in Edith's lap?

"You're good...sit."

Edith noticed his awkwardness and giggled.

"I'm here on your behalf. Don't look so surprised, Lily. It makes you seem like a mawkish owl. I am here to give you advice and aid. If you want it, that is."

Wondering what Edith could possibly be offering, my suspicions already having me shake my head in the negative, I stopped short when her following words registered, and I too sat down—hard.

"I am here to offer my services and help you get through the labyrinth in the lower levels of the forbidden library. You see, I've already been there. Twice, as a matter of fact."

* * *

LORCAN and I were snuggled on the sofa a few hours later. We ordered pizza and awaited its arrival by getting in some serious necking. Always good for the appetite, that. While I enjoyed our kissing session, I found my mind wandering back to what Edith imparted on me before I finally convinced her to leave, and I mean convince. Edith was so sure Lorcan was about to get naked and wanted to gaze at his incredible physique—after all, it was all hard, lean muscle. I informed her, however, that I wasn't as loose and fast, and she and my cousin Nora and *no* naked men would be forthcoming for her ogling pleasure. She had seemed disappointed and left soon after.

Come to think of it, Lorcan appeared a little glum as well.

"Earth to Lily. Come in, Lily."

"Sorry. Lorcan, I am just thinking about what Edith said. How did she get past the blood requirement? Do you think I should trust her?"

Lorcan gave my lips one last disheartened glance, then sighed and stretched. He regarded me a moment before speaking but then leaned forward with his hands on his knees.

"Lily. You told me yourself that she came in here carrying on and warning you about Harvey Rosen. You have to give her credit for that, even begrudgingly. Just the fact she did makes me wonder if she's grown fond of you."

"Ugh! I don't need or want her to keep popping up in my life, though! Can't she understand that and make other ghost friends? There has to be more of them! Although the girl who haunted my landing is long gone ever since the police identified those skeletal remains. I still can't believe Sheriff Buford only reprimanded Brian for flubbing that so." And boy, was I sore over that omission on my former boyfriend's part.

"At first, I thought he said Gordon Delany did the test, but then I realized it couldn't have been him—he wasn't here yet. When I asked the sheriff, he told me Brian had the testing sent to Gwinnett and the lovely Yolanda. She was the one who didn't bother being thorough and assumed it was

Deanna Fredricks based on what we told her. I could strangle that woman."

"You wouldn't be this upset because Brian is dating her, would you?" Lorcan kept his voice light with fake disinterest, but I could tell he needed to hear me tell him otherwise.

"Lor, you know I got the Brian infatuation out of the way and just disliked Yolanda because she's a catty snot-booger."

Barking out a laugh, Lorcan leaned forward and gave me a quick lip smack, then stood.

"I hear tires on gravel. That must be our pizza. Hold that thought. I want to hear more of this snot-booger person." Just then, the front doorbell gonged, and Lorcan headed out of the kitchen to get our food. I may have watched his derriere as he passed by. He did fill out those jeans rather well.

"I feel your eyes on me, you hussy!"

Giggling to myself, I went to wash my hands and get us some paper plates and napkins. This time I thought sitting in the sunroom would be an excellent delineation from our usual lounging in the den. I still hadn't purchased a kitchen table and wondered what happened to the one that used to be here before my mom, um, Aunt Jessica, took off with me.

I was having a difficult time wrapping my head around the Jessica, Adelaide, and Charlie equation. The only mom I'd ever known was Jessica Croy. I still can't imagine the sacrifice she made, giving up her life's dreams to pretend she was Charlie's wife and my mother. The family was as perplexed as I was, and we couldn't fathom the reason behind the deception. It must be a doozy.

However, on sleepless nights when my mind went into overdrive, I remembered glimpses of living here in the house in that time between wakefulness and dropping off to sleep. One memory had been niggling the recesses of my mind, and I recalled it now. I must have just celebrated my third

Birthday and was whining about not being permitted to have another piece of cake before bed. I shuffled over to Adelaide and rested my head on her knee.

"Mommy, make Jess give me another, prease? Pree prease?"

Obviously, I hadn't fully developed my speech yet.

"Lily! Remember what we told you. Call me Aunt Addy. Jessica is your mommy for now. Just for a little while, darling. OK? I know you don't understand. But you must be a bright girl and try hard."

"Will you give me more cake if I do?"

Laughing in delight, the bewitching young Adelaide clapped her hands and cupped my chin, grinning at my face.

"Yes, my darling. Let us go sneak another piece now before Jess and Charlie come back in, why don't we?"

"Ahem. I asked would you like a beer? Soda? You went away again there, Lily." Lorcan placed the pizza box on the table, opening the smaller box on top. It had six garlic rolls inside, dripping with olive oil and cheese. I guessed our kissing session was on hold for the time being.

"Sorry. Again. Yes. A Pepsi, please."

Lorcan shuddered a bit but grabbed my offensive beverage and a beer for himself. We were in Coke country, Atlanta being the birthplace of the carbonated drink. But I was a Pepsi girl, through and through, especially since I could get the real sugar version and not the icky corn syrup concoction, I detested.

"I was sitting here recalling another memory from when I was a little girl. Lorcan, I remembered calling Adelaide mommy. She told me not to, but to try and remember, just for a bit longer, it seems, that I was to call Jessica, mom, instead. What the heck was going on with those three? Will we ever find out?"

"We will if you and Adriana can figure out how to get Adelaide and Wicked separated."

We dug into our pizza—half pepperoni for Lorcan, plain

cheese for me—and ate without speaking for one slice each. Then we slowed down and began to discuss our relationship woes in between bites on our next piece.

"I have had so much going on lately, but that's no excuse, and I want to clear up some things with you. I shouldn't have put it off. Tonight, is a perfect time to talk, tomorrow you will have your family over, and I have some things I need to do early—way early in the morning—that I've been neglecting," began Lorcan, as he contemplated the third slice of pizza.

"I guess Andrea told you about the Tribunal. Lily, I don't want you to think I have changed my mind about where we are heading. It's just that, OK, here is the thing. Remember when I told you about Nora and me? Dating?"

I nodded yes, and suddenly I didn't like where this was going.

"OK, well, I may have left out that we went from going steady to being kind of engaged, and, well, that registry is still in the Tribunal, making us a betrothed couple. We never got around to taking it off the books."

It took everything in me not to smash my half-eaten pizza in Lorcan's face. Instead, I threw it as hard as I could across the room, where it slammed up against the wall and slid to the floor. Wicked was only too happy to gobble up some cheese that dropped with it.

Lorcan? He had some 'splaining to do.

CHAPTER 6

Sunday morning came, and I was still stewing. I didn't give Lorcan time to explain and sent him home, dejected and begging me to listen to reason. I, however, was totally in love with irrational and wanted to have a massive pity party and eat ice cream. Tubs of ice cream. I hate ice cream. I was still so distraught I did the only thing I knew to do. Call Andrea on the phone.

"What are you up to?"

"Nothing yet, Lily. It's, um...very early. What's wrong?" I could hear her stifle a yawn.

"Oh, nothing. I just tossed Lorcan out of my house last night. Now I want to go stalk him."

That comment was met with silence.

I waited a few more seconds. When Andrea failed to respond, I continued, "So... you with me, or what?"

Still, no reaction, and I was getting impatient.

"OK, if you don't want to come with me, I will go rent a car. I can't stalk him in George. Lorcan knows that truck better than I do."

George was my old Ford pickup truck on its last legs, so I always walked everywhere around town.

"Whoa! Hang on a minute, Lily. You...why? I mean, what the heck happened last night, anyway?"

"Nora," I growled.

"Nora came *over*? I don't understand."

I gave my response through gritted teeth, "Nora did not come *over*. Lorcan told me he and Nora were once engaged and they are still on the record books at this Tribunal thing."

"I'll be right over."

That's my girl.

I hung up my phone and rolled over in bed, and almost squashed a prostrate Wicked. Her eyes were barely open, just slits, but she still managed to give me the stink-eye. I reached my hand out to pet her, but she skooched over out of my reach.

Fine. After the cheese treat last night, too. Ungrateful beast.

Hopping out of bed, I tossed on some clothing and stared in the bathroom mirror. Hmm...I looked a bit crazed but decided some makeup and twisting my hair up in a sloppy bun would conceal my insanity—a bit.

I glanced at my phone to see the weather prediction and groaned when I saw rain was coming in, bringing a slight warming trend with it. That could mean anything from twenty-eight degrees to fifty-eight degrees or something in between in a matter of hours: layering, Lily. Get on layers and get a move on. Andrea was a quick dresser and would be pulling in any minute now.

Not knowing what Lorcan would be up to this morning, I opted for hiking boots and added a knit cap, scarf, and open finger gloves. There. That should get me through any situation. I hoped.

I gave Wicked fresh water and kibble downstairs in the

kitchen and noticed she'd gnawed through the last slice of pizza I had left on the table in the sunporch. There goes my breakfast. I didn't want to see anyone in town and have to explain, so I dug through an unpacked box in my pantry that I knew held travel mugs and, once I found them, brewed a pot of coffee so we'd have that at least.

While waiting on the pot to finish brewing, I heard Andrea's car pull into my driveway.

I unlocked the back door and went back to my task and had just filled both tumblers when Andrea knocked and walked in.

"You're crazy, but I am a willing accomplice. It gets me out of church anyway, and I'm not working in the bakery. Stevie is. However, I stopped in and got us treats."

I had already run over to Andrea when I saw she was carrying a few bags from the café and threw my arms around her in grateful, joyous glee. I almost swooned when I opened one and spied an array of yummy wonderfulness, knowing food-wise we had everything.

"How do you know when Lorcan is expected to leave anyway? And where is he going?"

"I don't know where he is going. Lorcan said he had things he needed to settle today that he'd been putting off and was evasive about it. I am going to follow him and see if his thing is Nora."

Realization dawned in Andrea's eyes, but then she frowned.

"But how do you know what time he'll head out?"

Just then, we heard a loud bang then a whizzing sound echo around my kitchen. I stared at Andrea and grinned.

"Adriana taught me that one. She used to spell my truck and scare the snot out of me every few days when I'd start him up. I figured out the spell was like an alarm to let her know I'd set it off. I also learned I could make it silent on one end while it sounded on the other. Lorcan just started his truck. Let's hurry and catch up to him."

"What if we lose him?" Andrea asked.

"Can't—tracking spell. Let's roll."

It was easy staying far back enough so Lorcan wouldn't spot us. Andrea had just purchased a Subaru Outback that was in the beige and green tones and didn't stand out, but we didn't want him to glance back and be able to see us through the windshield. We managed, however, as I had cast that spell with a bit of a tracking element and barely noticeable blue sparkles were trailing from Lorcan's exhaust.

Even though it was surprisingly busy out on the road for a Sunday morning, all those early bird churchgoers rushing about, we could easily stay behind him with that twinkling trail guiding us. Even better was the fact that only I could see it, so it didn't draw notice.

Lorcan was driving east out of town, and I felt my stomach sink when I realized he was heading toward the small home Deputy Gordon Delaney, Nora's boyfriend and where she'd been living these last few months, had been renting. I was about to tell Andrea to speed up so we could honk, and I could give Lorcan a one-fingered salute, but he kept driving past the place and got on the highway that led to Clayton. OK, then. Sit back, and let's see where this is going.

Andrea and I were sipping coffee and munching our incredible breakfast treats, slightly bleary-eyed. But with eighties tunes playing on her subscription channel, our mood was fairly jovial. We were singing along with Depeche Mode, and I wondered again at how lucky I was to find the one cousin out of my massive family who had the same taste as me, and that would be a constant and reliable companion to my hair-brained schemes. Andrea did this without too much question, and I was so happy we were the best of friends, as well.

"Andrea, can't you hit us with one of your cloaking spells, so we disappear and Lorcan won't see us?"

"Ah, that's not a good idea. You see, we are driving out of Sweet Briar. So, once we arrive wherever he's heading, what then? We park and I cast it somewhere out of the way? It's magic that requires tons of spellcasting strength. I don't have all my jewelry on that would bolster my powers to make us completely disappear. And can you imagine if a human happens by and catches us? One minute we are there and the next, poof? Gone?"

She had a point.

We arrived in Clayton, and Lorcan stopped at a parts store. Innocuous so far, but hardly something he would 'put off,' as he stated. We pulled into a gas station next door and parked on the side of the building, which still gave us a good vantage point, but kept us reasonably hidden.

Twenty minutes later, Lorcan came out of the store balancing two medium-sized boxes and put them in the bed of his truck. We pulled out of the service station, keeping a safe distance behind Lorcan, and followed him to his next destination. A hardware store.

A hardware store? Wasn't our friend Dennis Carter's good enough? What could he possibly need at a hardware store in Clayton that he couldn't get at Dennis' shop in Sweet Briar?

Lorcan was in there for thirty minutes, and when he came out, he only had a receipt in his hand. Interesting, but nothing that would seem like he'd delay doing it no matter what my brain was imagining.

The next stop was a barbershop that was old-fashioned complete with one of those turning red, white and blue thingamajigs outside mounted on the wall. We watched Lorcan go in and head to the counter where he stood for only a few minutes, then turn around and come out walking over to the passenger side of his truck. He opened the door and pulled out what looked like a white sack filled with clothes. Suddenly, he removed his jacket, then stripped off his sweatshirt, revealing hard, rippling muscles that stopped traffic.

No, really.

Three women, all in separate vehicles, slammed on their brakes when they noticed his physique. I couldn't help but smile and enjoy the view, and *what* a view. I was rendered speechless, which is saying a lot. I had no idea that *that* is what Lorcan had been hiding under his shirt. Even Andrea was dumbstruck until I poked her side.

"Wow. I guess you build up some amazing muscles working on all those cars all day, huh?"

"What's he doing now? I mean, it is pretty chilly out there, and he's...oh."

Lorcan pulled another sweatshirt on and tucked the one he was wearing into the sack at his feet. Then he shut his truck door and went into a laundromat next door to the barbershop. We could see him go up to a machine, load his clothing into the washer, and then start it. Back outside, he continued past his truck and into the barbershop once more.

This time we waited...and waited...

"I need to pee."

Andrea was squirming, and I looked around for somewhere she could take care of business without us having to leave our observation post. There was nothing on our side of the parking lot, so I sighed and drove over to a McDonald's, begging her to hurry. She did, then I took my turn, and we were back into position in time to see Lorcan return to the laundromat, then sit around and wait for another fifteen minutes for his clothes to finish. He put them into the dryer, then left and got into his truck. I guessed he was going someplace while they dried and told Andrea to get ready to follow.

"Oh my gosh! Andrea, Lorcan is pulling into that jewelry store. Hurry, go around the back."

Andrea parked and we tried to see if he went inside to no avail. We either had to risk going around the front, doing a casual drive-by hoping he didn't see us, or I had to sneak around the side of the building on foot and peek in the window, hoping we didn't come face to face. I noticed a Jeep dealership next door and took note of the layout of the jewelry store reflecting in its huge windows. The jewelry store had two darkened side windows and front windows on either side of the entry door. I was unsure what was on the other side of the building, but I assumed a similar setup.

"I'm getting out. We can't risk a drive-by. Please do me a favor and turn around, pointing to this rear parking area. You'll be able to gun it through the back lot and duck around that building next door, so we'd lose him."

"You want me to go to..."

"No time...just do it, OK?"

Andrea frowned, but nodded letting me know she under-stood what I meant, I hoped, and I slipped out of her car and slowly crept along the side of the jewelry store. I glanced back at her once to make sure she was in position, then pulled in a deep breath and peered into one of the windows. I was observed a rather large store but could see Lorcan, his back to me, thankfully, peering at something a rather fetching blonde was showing him. She kept laughing at something he was saying and playing with her hair.

I hated her on sight.

Especially when she touched his arm, then felt it again. OK, one more touch and I was going to...

Duck!

Lorcan turned suddenly, almost as if he could feel my eyes boring into the back of his head. Oh my gosh! What if he spied me? I squat walked as fast as I could around the back of the building and over to Andrea's...nothing. No Andrea! Not a car in sight. Looking around frantically, I noticed Lorcan walk out of the jewelry store because he was now being reflected in the Jeep dealership's windows as well. Great.

If he glanced in that direction, he'd notice me standing behind the building. I tore around the other side of the store and stopped short when I saw him spin around and head back to their front door. That's when he looked up, and I flattened myself against the wall, then turned, running like an imbecile into the woods behind the shop.

I could hear him call out but kept running, turning left, and hitting the fence that surrounded the dealership—not even thinking. Like seriously? Had I been using my brain cells all this time? Uh...*no*. I climbed the fence, grateful it did not have razor wire across the top. Dropping down into the back lot, I tore off at an insane pace, raced through the service department, flung open the doors to the repair section, and startled about fifteen mechanics, then flew through the door on the opposite side.

It led to a breakroom of sorts, and I kept going, opening doors until I found myself in the showroom. That's when I saw Andrea driving around slowly outside as if she was searching for a place to park. I was going to strangle her.

Trying to appear nonchalant, I walked over to the big showroom window and glanced over to the jewelry store. Lorcan was walking in this direction.

"May I help you?"

"Jesus!" I shrieked.

"Ma'am? My name is Dewayne. Not Jesus."

What? I had no *time* for this.

"Can I help you?" The youngish in appearance salesman looked askance at me as I gripped his arm and all but screeched.

"Jeep! I need a Jeep. Let's go in here!" Dragging him into the nearest cubicle, I sat down and began to rock back and forth.

"I'm sorry...is there something wrong?"

"No...um...Dewayne..." I regarded his crooked tie then tracked up to his eyes, noticing how startled he was by my demeanor. "I would just like to see some Jeeps and hope you have a brochure I could take with me?" I added a smile—all teeth—that I hoped would reassure the young man, but it only seemed to make him back up a bit; although he tried not to let on, he was nervous as he moved away.

"Wouldn't you rather go outside and test drive one? Or at least walk around one?"

"No! No. I just need a brochure and, holy Batman!" Lorcan was suddenly in the waiting area attached to the showroom, just off the service drive. If he turned and peered at all the cubicles, he was sure to discover me cowering.

"Yes! A test drive! Let's go on a *test* drive now. Hurry, Dewayne....please."

I flew out of the cubicle, not glancing back, and ran out the dealership's front door onto the lot. Andrea, the trai-torous shrew, was once again in the back of the jewelry store, and I could see she was scratching her head.

Dewayne rushed out behind me and stopped short when he realized I wasn't moving.

"Uh...do you have a model preference? Color? Four-door? Two?" I had to give him credit; he wasn't going to let my insanity stop him from trying his best to land a deal.

I peered behind me and was relieved to see Lorcan had not followed, which meant he was probably still around back. I had to try and get over to Andrea, but that way meant possible detection. I contemplated my earnest salesman again and smiled once more.

"Do you have the keys to that orange one there? I will go

wait by it if you run and get them. It's perfect!" Dewayne's eyes lit up when he saw I was pointing at a Jeep Wrangler, a Rubicon model, four doors and loaded to the max in a gorgeous burnt orange. His entire face transformed with a massive grin, and he told me to wait then tore off back into the dealership to fetch the keys.

I headed over to the Jeep and ducked down behind it, trying to see if I could spot Lorcan anywhere outside the property and hoped he'd decided he imagined seeing me skulking around and went back to the jewelers. At this point, he'd probably notice Andrea sitting in her car behind the building, and the game would be up.

"Um, ma'am? Would you like to get in?"

"Oh! Dewayne. Yes, uh, sure." I snatched the key out of his hand and unlocked the Jeep. Once in, I wasted no time fiddling at knobs or waiting for Dewayne's salesman speak on what was what. I turned that sucker on and pulled out of the parking spot, and all but gunned it over to Andrea's Subaru.

"Andrea. *Andrea!*" I honked, startling her so that she jumped back and bumped her head. Looking way up—the Jeep had some wicked tires that made it much higher than the little wagon—Andrea opened her mouth in a perfect *O* when she noticed me. Then she glanced behind me, and her eyes widened. I didn't have to turn around to comprehend Lorcan must be heading in our direction. Instead, I stared at Dewayne and said, "Hang on, kid."

I peeled out of the parking lot and tore down the main highway, not stopping until I was about four miles down the road and pulled into a small parking area with what looked like...

"Are those goats up there? On the *roof?*"

"Um...yeah. This here place has a deli and ice cream and,

well, as you can see, they keep goats on the roof as a tourist attraction."

"But why on the roof?"

"Don't know ma'am... you'd hafta ask them goats." I searched Dewayne's face and he seemed serious.

I had no intention of getting out of this vehicle and approaching a cluster of very hungry-looking goats. There was something so off-putting about their wiggy eyes. I didn't suspect they'd answer any query I put to them anyway.

Suddenly, Dewayne gulped and squeaked out, "Ma'am, you ain't crazy, right? I mean... it's my first day on the job, and I forgot to get a copy of your license and make sure you have insurance." He shook his head in amazement at his faux pas, then continued, a hitch in his voice, "I didn't see you come in with no car. And now, well, see? If I lose this job, my momma is going to be mighty upset. My daddy just passed a year back now, and I graduated high school, and now I am working in, what I hope, will bring good money back home so my momma can stop working two jobs. I got three more brothers, younger, and a baby sister too."

He gave me such a solemn gaze that I did what anyone in my situation would do. I started crying my eyes out.

That's why I am now the proud owner of a brand new Jeep.

* * *

"I DON'T WANT to talk about it."

"But Lily...let me explain."

"I don't want to talk about it, Andrea. Just head back to town. I will meet you at Joe's in about an hour."

"But...but Lorcan and, where *are* you?" Andrea sounded like she, too, was about to start bawling.

"I am sitting here with Dewayne...a nice young man, and I

am finalizing the purchase of my new Jeep. No. Andrea. Stop sputtering and listen to me. It's OK. Go back to Sweet Briar and I will meet you at Joe's." I hung up my cell phone and smiled at the young salesman who was now grinning like he just won the lottery. In a way, he had. Do you have any idea how much a fully loaded Rubicon is going for these days? I'd just about cleared out my savings account getting it, too. Dewayne would be earning quite the commission.

"And an all-cash deal. My word. If you had told me when I saw you running in here like some mad woman on a mission that you'd be buying this here car at full price *and* all cash? I never would have believed it. Momma is going to be so happy. She's gonna cry her eyes out."

She wouldn't be the only one.

I'd already taken a massive chunk out of my trust to repair my home. I had planned on buying a new car, but no way did I consider getting something this expensive. I'd be eating spaghetti and butter for months—years even—to try and make that money back. I had no intention of touching any Dolce funds, no matter *what* my family said.

"Just sign here. Now here. My, my, you are all done, Miz Sweet. Here are your keys!"

I had caused quite the commotion at the dealership, and more than one salesperson and even a few mechanics had come out to see me take possession of my new vehicle. Lorcan had apparently gone, and I wondered what he was thinking. Well, I could legitimately say I had every right to be in Clayton since I intended to purchase a car even if it was a bald-faced lie.

As I waved goodbye to the little farewell party of employees who waved back enthusiastically, I couldn't help but notice I had picked up one incredibly gorgeous ride. I mean, in my wildest dreams, I never saw myself behind the wheel of a Jeep. But ten minutes down the road and I knew I was falling in love faster than anyone had a right. I replaced dear old George with precisely what I'd been looking for— even before I knew I was looking for it.

"I think I am going to name you Gypsy." I purred, then messed with the knobs of the radio, thrilled when I realized I had a free subscription to satellite radio. Tuning it to the New Wave station, I sang along with my favorite eighties band as INXS came on, and Michael Hutchence cried out, "This Is What You Need."

Indeed, it is, Michael. Indeed, it is.

Pulling into the first gas station once I arrived back in the outskirts of Sweet Briar, I decided to top off the tank since the dealership had only half-filled her. Heading to the closest open spot, I parked and turned off my engine, then hopped out. That's when I noticed Harley Jacobs sitting in his truck one section over.

It was running, and it didn't appear he'd was used the gas pump. He was staring intently at the convenience store, and I glanced over my shoulder as I reached for my purse to grab a credit card, trying to ascertain what was so worth his concentration. Everything seemed normal to me, so I shrugged and continued with my task.

After making my purchase and choosing unleaded, I opened the gas tank and inserted the nozzle. Trying to tamp down my excitement at my excessive purchase, I found myself reaching out to pat my Jeep's side, grinning all the while. It really was a stunning vehicle. The promised rain had not materialized, and the sun was shining through the clouds onto the paint job. I could see fine gold flecks of metal in the burnt orange paint, making the Jeep sparkle. I hadn't even had her an hour, and I was smitten.

The automatic shut-off disengaged, letting me know my tank was now full, and I pulled the nozzle out, replacing it at the pump. That's when I noticed Harley hadn't moved and was still glowering at the store. What on earth was wrong with him? Walking over tentatively, I waved and called out to him. Nothing. It was like he was in a trance, not moving in the slightest, eyes fixed and vacant with a strange scowl on his very dead face.

Oh my gosh! He can't be!

But there was no mistaking it. Even with the door between him and me, it was obvious Harley Jacobs wouldn't be keeping any future appointments with Adriana and me. He'd be taking whatever information he had for us to his grave.

Why did I get out of bed this morning? *Why?*

CHAPTER 7

"You need to tell me again just what you were doing with the victim and why you showed up at the scene? It sounds to me like you were checking up on your crime of passion. I heard whispers of a nasty quarrel you had the other day with the deceased." Deputy Gordon Delaney had been going round and round with his idiotic questions for three-quarters of an hour now. Even though we had broken up before we had ever really gotten started, I was thrilled when Detective Brian Chase pulled into the service station.

"Deputy. Lily, are you OK?" I had to hand it to Brian. Lately, he'd been downright pleasant to me despite my pulling away from his intense courtship of sorts a few months back. He'd decided after a few weeks of dating that we were meant to be together and destined for a pair of dark witchlings of our own after walking down the aisle. Considering I had a love-hate relationship with small people that drooled and pooped in their pants, his declaration hadn't won me over. It did quite the opposite. It made me realize he was a tad overbearing and pushy, wrapped in a gorgeous package, mind you, but I had no intention of being pushed into something for which I wasn't ready.

We won't discuss the fact that I had been picturing little Lorcan's running around my family home for the last few weeks. Seriously. I'm not going to discuss it.

"I'm fine, Brian. I'm a bit rattled, but..."

"But it's not like you haven't already seen a bunch of dead bodies with your track record and all." Deputy Gordon had a sneer on his face and kept jingling his handcuffs like he was waiting for any excuse to slap them on me and haul me off to the pokey.

They say pokey a lot here in the South.

"You can forget about hauling me to the pokey and go process the scene or something, deputy. I had nothing to do with any of this, this horrible thing that happened to poor Harley."

"So, you say. So, you say. And I didn't mention any... what did you call it? Pokey? That might be your guilty conscience talking."

"That will be enough, deputy." Brian turned away from Gordon, who had a dark scowl cross his face that he all but managed to wipe clean when Brian regarded him once more. He addressed the deputy like he would a naughty child who had refused to listen after repeated instruction. "You heard the lady...go seal the scene and keep the looky-loo's away."

Dismissing Gordon like an annoying gnat, Brian focused all his attention on me. Those piercing azure-blue eyes inquisitive, professional yet with a hint of concern that made me feel like everything would be OK, and no one would haul me off to jail. At least not for the foreseeable future.

"What did Gordon mean a quarrel? Did you have a problem with Harley that I need to know about?"

I told Brian about my running into the street and almost getting myself smushed, then about how Harley had stomped over, looking all irate. Only to insinuate he had something important to discuss with Adriana and me and that it had to do with the Fredericks duo. This after he finished berating me for running out in front of him.

"Although how Gordon found out about it is beyond me. It's like Chad Barwick all over again, Brian. Harley told me he needed to discuss this thing with us, and now he's dead, and I found the body! I am not going to pretend this didn't rattle me. I am freaking out here."

Brian turned his head and scrutinized the deputy running crime scene tape hither and yon, then rubbed his chin. "I suspect the gossip mill had a gander at the two of you and misinterpreted what they saw. Easy to happen. You did say Harley came flying out of his truck, slamming the door all confrontational, before he told you he'd like a meeting of sorts." Brian returned his gaze to me and smiled, "I suspect Gordon found out from Nora. I heard her yammering over at the salon about you picking fights with everyone in town. She didn't mention Harley by name, but the timeline fits."

Of course, it would be Cousin Nora.

"What were you doing at the salon?" I asked, realizing I crossed into dangerous territory when I saw the quick blush creep up Brian's neck. That had to mean one thing, he either met Yolanda, his current girlfriend, and a medical examiner there or brought her to get her hair or nails done. Why couldn't that woman stay in Gwinnett County where she belonged? Hold on. What if...no, that would be too much.

"Please tell me Yolanda and Nora haven't become BFFs...I don't think I could handle another pair of mean girls picking at me for no apparent reason."

Brian had the grace to look abashed, but it wasn't winning any brownie points with me. After all, he was the one kissing on dear Yolanda barely a day after professing his undying love for our unborn children and me. I had every right to be offended and hold this grudge.

"I am not a fan of your cousin, but trust me...I had nothing to do with the two of them bonding."

Oh please. Spare me the excuses.

"Detective! You may want to come here a minute." A deputy from the state patrol that worked with Brian was standing near the open door of Harley's truck. He was still sitting in the same position, staring across the parking lot in a fierce macabre way, like he'd have a choice in the matter. Brian rushed over, and the two officers conferred a moment. Then Brian gazed back over to me, frowning.

Uh oh. I did not have a good feeling about this.

I had to wait another few minutes while both men went through the motions of bagging something as evidence. Brian said a few more parting words to the deputy who tipped his hat then went over to his squad car, driving off with whatever he had found. At least I thought he did. I wouldn't say I liked how Brian stood staring at the dead man as the lone EMT and my good friend, Shirley Jones, stood by having words with him. She was shaking her head in the negative and even stomped her foot a time or two. What could they possibly be arguing about?

Shirley pointed to Harley then said a few more things to Brian, which made him scrutinize the body before shaking his head and shrugging. A few words carried over to me, and I could just make out Shirley asking, "What else could it be though, can you be paralyzed to death? You need to ask your girlfriend to clarify when she gets here because I don't know what to write in my report."

Brian nodded his head, then turned and walked over to me with an unreadable mien on his face. I could tell Shirley wanted to come over and speak with me, but Brian must have forbidden her from doing so.

"What is it? What did that deputy find?" I asked, holding my breath in anticipation of the answer he would give me.

Taking out his phone, Brian swept across a few photos until he found what he'd been searching for, then he turned the screen to face me.

"Recognize this?"

I stared at the photo, which showed a medium-sized, bronze-colored glass bottle with a cork stopper.

"It looks like a potion bottle of some sort...but no, I don't recognize it per se."

Brian considered my words for just a moment, and then he swiped across his screen once more.

"This was found clutched in Harley's hand along with the potion bottle."

I glanced down at the screen and felt my blood run cold. Harley had been holding a small piece of paper, more like a label of some sort. Scribbled on it were five words: A Gift from Miss Sweet.

"Ohmygosh! Oh no! Brian. I didn't. It wasn't me. I wasn't even here! I told you. Check! Call everyone. Call Dewayne. Andrea! Oh, my goodness!"

Brian's eyes widened, and he held up his hands before trying to get a word in. I wasn't making it easy. "Lily...whoa! Hey! Stop! Will you hush?"

I stopped, but I was breathing hard and trying not to hyperventilate.

"I told you I already checked out you and Andrea's timeline. Steve didn't know why I was calling and confirmed Andrea was there early to pick up pastries, and then he saw the two of you drive by in Andrea's car around eight.

"You passed by this station a little after that because Donald and Doreen saw you and Andrea driving by...heard you, too, it seems. I guess you were singing loudly with the radio cranked. Anyway, when they saw the commotion over here and you standing off waiting for us to inspect the scene of the crime, Doreen called the station and told dispatch your whereabouts this morning. They had been out painting the shutters on the motel and saw Harley drive by about two hours ago. I just finished speaking to dispatch as I pulled in just now.

"I will call the dealership and verify your whereabouts and a timeline for that. Rest easy, girl. Shirley gave me her estimate for a time of death, but until Yol...um, the medical examiner, uh...Yolanda gets here; I won't have an official estimate for the time of death. Or the cause of death, for that matter. But even I know you were nowhere near Harley today. You've been cleared."

Other than hearing Yolanda's name, yet again, causing me to scowl, my nerves were finally at the breaking point, and I'd had more than I could take. When Brian informed me I wasn't under suspicion, I did the one thing I seemed to be good at today. I burst out in fresh tears.

"Oh, hey now. Stop. Lily, stop!" Brian started patting me and looked uncomfortable enough that I laugh-cried for a second, but then I just lost it with the stress of the day and went all-out bawling. Hey! I am a girl. Occasionally, I am entitled to pull out my chick card and use it with abandon.

Brian wasn't quite sure what to do with such a blubbering mess, so he wrapped me up in a comforting hug and stroked the back of my hair while whispering, "there, there...you let it out. It will be OK, you'll see."

I cried myself out pretty quick and went from tears to hiccuping short breaths and pulled away slightly. Brian wasn't letting me completely escape his arms, however.

"You OK?"

I nodded yes.

"Good. I promise I will get to the bottom of this. I mean it." Brian stared deeply into my eyes and I knew the minute it went from a friendly, comforting shoulder to lean on to a man who wanted much more, and I instantly began to pull away, knowing this was wrong on so many levels. That's when he leaned forward and gave me a quick kiss on the lips, his hands on either side of my face.

It would have ended right there since I had begun to push him away, but that was also when we heard a car approaching. Turning at the same time, we saw Yolanda Serrano pulling into the station, a grimace of supreme ire on her face. Seriously. If looks could kill, I would be a splat of bubbling goo from the laser beams she was sending in my direction. I heard Brian groan a smidge, then sigh in resignation.

And even more disturbing, I just happened to glance past her to see Lorcan at the curb, one leg out of his truck, mouth hanging open. My stomach dropped. I raised my hand in a pathetically weak greeting, a half-hearted attempt to make it seem perfectly normal to be in the arms of my ex-boyfriend, who had just had his lips pressed to mine, and that I was glad to see my current boyfriend...and wasn't this nice?

Oh, no.

This was not going to be pleasant.

Especially since, right then, Lorcan chose to get back into his truck, slam the door and turn on the engine. Then, tires squealing, he sped off back down the highway toward Sweet Briar.

This time, it appeared I had some 'splaining to do!

* * *

I WAS BANGING MY HEAD.

I was banging my head over and over on the table in my sunporch. Andrea was rubbing her hand up and down across my back, murmuring words of comfort.

It didn't stop me from banging my head. Over and over.

I had food catered in from Joe's arriving tonight since I wasn't up to cooking spaghetti for the relatives. Everyone would be here in about an hour, but there I was. I was banging my head on the table and moaning.

"Lily! Will you stop that now. Oh, honey. Look at what you are doing to yourself."

I stopped and sat up, peering at Andrea through my bangs. She gazed up at my forehead, which may or may not have a sugar packet stuck to it. Hey, it's sweaty work banging your head over and over on a table.

Andrea reached up and peeled the sugar packet away and smoothed my bangs off my face. "Oh, girl. What am I going to do with you?"

"Shoot me? Andrea, what have I done? You should have seen the grimace on Lorcan's face. I was practically making out right there in front of a dead Harley Jacobs for everyone to see. And Lorcan looked like a kicked puppy." Right before his face got stormy and he hightailed it out of Dodge, that is.

"He will get over it. It's not like he can talk--not removing both of their names off the Tribunal register--don't let him make you feel like you did anything wrong. It was Brian being Brian again. You were pushing him away. You were pushing him away, right?"

"Of course, I was pushing him away! I don't want to lead him on and make more of a mess! I want to be with Lorcan and only Lorcan. He caught me totally by surprise with that kiss."

Andrea pondered the entire sordid tale a minute, then continued, "I wonder why the guy working in the convenience store didn't notice poor old Harley out there just sitting at the pump not doing anything. Why didn't he go check on him?"

"Brian told me the guy is a lazy old pothead and he wouldn't care one bit if all the customers came in then dropped dead in the parking lot. Then again, Harley did not just drop dead. He drank that potion on his own, or someone made him drink it. He either committed suicide or someone murdered him. But who would kill him, and why? What was he about to tell me?"

And not a camera in sight, either. The owners hadn't updated that old gas station since the early nineties and it didn't have any surveillance. A few hundred feet up the road, Doreen and Donald's motel had their cameras pointing this way, but could barely make out the one side of the lot that the gas station was on. And it couldn't see the pumps where we had parked. However, Brian was getting the feed to have a visual record of us leaving town, Harley entering the town and pulling into the gas station, then me showing up an hour later and pulling in near him. At least I had an iron-clad alibi, thanks to my Jeep-purchasing fiasco.

"Oh my! The Jacobs! I assume Brian or Sheriff Buford has gone over to inform them. Those poor people. Harley was their only child. Who is going to help with the farm now?" Andrea worried her bottom lip, "I hope they won't have to sell it."

I hoped not either—what a mess.

"I need to call June. She will know when it is proper to go over with a casserole and offer our condolences."

Something I was not remotely good at, being the daughter of a hermit. Or...er...niece. Jessica, my Aunt Jessica, lived so secluded, afraid of the bad guys. With all that happened in my life as of late, it seemed Jessica Croy was correct in her worrying. There seems to be an inordinate amount of malice following me around ever since I'd arrived. Well, if you consider Donna Fredericks being the instigator of evil on my small family. I'd been a victim of these goings-on for years!

"Andrea. This time I am not waiting for Adriana or

Susanne Washington to come blasting in and save the day. This time, I control my magic and won't be knocking myself out cold, relying on others to swoop in and figure out how to control a bad situation. This time I am going to solve Harley Jacobs's murder all by myself. With your help, that is."

My name is Lily Sweet, dark witch and amateur sleuth on a mission. And you can put that in your pipe and smoke it.

CHAPTER 8

"*D*o I seem like someone who has time to worry about a stupid book and guardian Sentinels? I have a murder to solve!" I had been trying for the better three-quarters of an hour to convince my relatives that I had more important things to do right now, and we needed to bench the forbidden library quest for the time being.

Plus, I had a feeling whoever killed Harley Jacobs would have a hand in what had been going on around here for decades. I wondered if Donna was somehow controlling this person. Or vice versa. It's the only thing that made sense. Harley informed me he had information. Someone must have seen the interchange on Friday and was worried enough they killed Harley. Or someone heard about it and killed him.

This person had also gotten into Rowan Nightingale's head, possessing her and making her kill Edith Plank, after all. Someone messed up at the prison and now Donna was running wild in its many caverns, not able to escape, we assumed, but I had no faith in the Council. There were so many unanswered questions and roadblocks in my quest to end this diabolical mission to destroy my family that I couldn't seem to keep it all in order. This explains why I was trying to get the family to focus on my need to solve Harley's murder rather than following Adriana's advice about getting into the library.

Adriana, of course, was having a blast playing Devil's Advocate. Every time I had the room convinced investigating Harley's murder made sense, she'd bring up "poor Adelaide" being stuck in a cat and set everyone off again. Only to reel it back when someone pointed out I'd be taking my life in my hands trying to get a spell and flee from Sentinels. Then she'd muse aloud the verity of my suggestion that whoever killed Harley had to be behind everything we'd gone through, and it was on again in earnest. I was about to knock her off the stool she was perched on like a demonic bat. Every time someone else blew up in frustration, she'd cackle like the dark witch she was.

This was going nowhere fast.

I was about to continue making my argument when Edith Plank chose that moment to pop up and ruin dinner. Really. She came up through the meatloaf and mashed potatoes, and I felt my stomach lurch from the vision.

"Edith! What are you doing here?"

Everyone in the room, and that was a goodly portion of my family and friends, fell silent. Present were Aunt Chiara and Uncle Steven with Steve Junior and Andrea. Aunt Iona, Uncle Owen, and Doug sat across from them around the table. Grandpa Antonio and Adriana on one end and June, Dennis, and Jake Carter on my side. Becky Dolan was next to Jake since they were becoming quite the couple. Cousin Sophia Valentina was here minus Sebastiano and Flora. The only glaring omission was the Reid's, Henry, Eileen, and Lorcan. Eileen had called and said Lorcan had informed her he'd not be attending tonight, and she sent her regrets.

Oh. This other woman was sitting in the corner near me, nodding her head. She looked familiar, but I couldn't seem to place her. I vaguely wondered if she was the lady that had been with Sophia a few weeks back and was a cousin of some sort or another aunt. Or maybe she was just a friend. I really couldn't keep any more people than these present straight, for heaven's sake! However, she wasn't ringing any; *hey, I just met you and forgot your name,* bells, so perhaps not. She appeared more Scot and could hardly be a Dolce with that faded red hair.

Leaning over in sotto voice, she whispered, "That will certainly put ye off your meal, no?" Nodding toward the center of the table where Edith had manifested in the meat-loaf, then she leaned back, chuckling in an eerily familiar way. Yep, a Scot, and one that could see ghosts!

Everyone began asking questions in which Adriana played center stage, which in turn had Edith whisking over to her side to berate her for one thing or the other. So, I chose to lean toward the older woman who just made that proclamation and asked, "I'm sorry...I, um...can you see Edith's ghost?"

"What kind o' dark witch would I be if I couldnae see her? O' course, I kin see her, what a silly question. What I'd like tae know is why haven't ye told anyone aboot me? And what's more, how come you kin see me, and hear me, but Adriana cannot?"

That's when I understood the woman sitting by my side was, herself, a ghost.

Oh, this night was going to be a memorable one. I just knew it.

* * *

AFTER EVERYONE HAD CLEARED OUT, for the most part, I was left in a confused daze, sitting by the fire in the living room. With me was Adriana, Andrea, Jake and Becky. Grandpa Antonio had hitched a ride home with his granddaughter, my Aunt Chiara.

As he left, he pulled me into a gentle hug and informed me I was, "Sei una brava ragazza." A good girl. Patting me on the head, he told me that I had a high fat optimus lava standing in my house and made Adriana happy. He didn't say or mean that, but that's what it sounded like in his half English, mostly Italian speak. So, I just nodded and kissed him on both cheeks, sending him on his merry way. Someday soon, I needed a crash-course in Italian. Just what the heck did hai fatto mean, anyway? I was getting a complex about my weight!

"That was a monumental waste of time. My aunts want me safe and refuse to consider me doing this Sentinel run you insist I do. Nor do they want me looking into the Harley Jacobs murder or possible suicide. Both my uncles are trying to stay on the good side of their wives so they agreed with them, and Steve Junior got his ear tweaked when he said I should do whatever I felt needed doing."

"I thought your Aunt Iona was going to pitch a fit when my mom said Adelaide could wait a bit longer inside that cat, and nothing much could be done until the Council finishes examining that dagger anyway. It's been making the rounds in secret with only the most trusted Elders trying to figure out why there seems to be fresh blood on it." Andrea stated.

"Maybe that stupid cat kept stabbing herself with it. I'd think her blood and Adelaide's mixed in some way. Look at her, trying to sneak a drink out of my mug. Shoo! Crazy cat." Adriana gave my sleek, black feline a dark scowl which only garnered a dismissive gaze and a tail swish in return from Wicked.

"My mom and dad stayed out of it. In any case, mom just wants you safe, but she knows you need those answers that are in that book. I thought it endearing when she suggested someone else volunteer to run through the labyrinth and get it instead of you." Jake stated, leaning back putting his arm around Becky. Her flaxen hair spread out in a halo of pale gold and she was blinking lazily at everyone in the room, her eyes glassy. Today was supposed to be her day off, and here she was stuck at my house with my crazy family yelling and carrying on for hours.

"In any case, I think it fascinating that you say Edith had crossed through the forbidden library twice. I don't know how she pulled that off, but we have to give her some credit for offering to help you get through it." Jake finished.

"More coffee, anyone?" I had been steadfastly trying to ignore the older lady sitting in the dining room, now knitting herself a ghostly shawl. Edith was still here but refused to look at or speak to me. I was OK with that, although I didn't know why her nose was out of joint. I did find it odd that she seemed aware of the other ghost but refused to acknowledge her presence. Even weirder still was Adriana's total lack of knowledge that an old ghost was sitting just behind her, laughing at every snarky comment she'd made tonight.

"Me!" Jake's hand shot in the air, as did Andrea's. Becky just groaned and rolled over onto her side, pulling a toss pillow over her head.

"None for me, cara. But if you can bring me some water?" Adriana asked politely, rare for her.

As I hurried back into the kitchen to refill the coffee mugs and grab Adriana a glass of water, my eyes tracked to the den and a wall of family photos my parents had on display.

Hey now! Wait a minute.

Setting the glass down on the counter, I wandered over and perused the faces. It didn't take me long to find a younger version of the elderly ghost in quite a few of the photos. I knew I'd seen her! In one, she held a baby me while my Aunt Adelaide, uh mom, looked on. In another, she was sitting in the sunporch, saying something to a laughing Adelaide while my dad, Charlie, and my mom, uh, Aunt Jessica, were passing me between them. I had my hand outstretched and was trying to grab whatever the woman had in her hand.

The last photo was of me at about four, and it must have been close to the time we ran away. I was sitting in the woman's lap, and she was reading me a story.

I took the photo off the wall and brought it over to my guests.

"Can anyone here tell me who this woman is, please?" I held the photo out, and Adriana snatched it, albeit gently, out of my hand.

"That's your Great Aunt Moira. May she rest in peace, dear woman. Your Grandmother Maggie's sister."

Oh, well, that explained the ghost, chuckling softly in my dining room and who must have been aiding and abetting Adelaide, Jessica, and whomever else was hiding trinkets for me to find all over this house. Because isn't she just now moving the placemat ever so slightly across the table? That means this ghost, at least, could manipulate matter, just like her granddaughter Ellie, come to think of it. It must be a family trait of some kind.

I'd met the twins, my Fortune cousins, Maggie—named after my grandmother, and her sister Ellie—back in January when their antique caravan had come through town with my Scottish grandparents in tow. Imagine my surprise when I discovered one of the cousins, Ellie, was a ghost! Her sister Maggie had reached her hand out to her sister, who'd grabbed and held on to it. So, Ellie, too, could touch matter, just like her grandmother, Moira. Interesting. I'd have to call Maggie and ask her about this.

"Oh! Your drinks." Running back to the kitchen with Andrea on my heels to help, I grabbed the glass of water off the counter, shooing Wicked away from it. Adriana need not know my cat had just been lapping some of it up—I certainly wouldn't tell her.

Setting the glass in front of her now, I asked the question that was bothering me ever since I noticed the specter.

"Why is she in so many photos? I don't remember her, but she seems to have been here several times." The older woman just smiled at my questions.

Adriana placed the photo on the coffee table and sat back again. "Moira would often travel between Scotland and the States. She used to visit your Croy, Muir, and Fortune relations for several weeks at a time. Then right after Addy disappeared, followed by your father, Moira, decided to rush over here and find out what had happened. I believe she hoped to speak with Jessica. It's a pity you don't remember her. You loved your great aunt, so."

Adriana paused, appearing forlorn, then continued. "She arrived one week too late. Jessica had run off with you. Moira stayed on and was an integral part of the search team. She was a Tracker, you see. After a week or so, she left word that she might have found a lead, but then we heard a horrible accident occurred. A spell Moira cast to find you backfired, and she was injured. That wasn't enough to do her fatal harm, but it made her a bit mad. She spent the next few weeks under a Cleric's care as they tried to figure out what had happened." My great-grandmother shivered a little and wrapped her shawl tightly to ward off the cold that only she could feel since the room was toasty warm.

"The next anyone heard, Moira Muir Fortune had taken a

draught of her making to remove the "malaise and sadness" from her mind. Instead, the potion she made killed her. We don't know if she mixed the wrong ingredients in her damaged state or if it was intentional. Poor Maggie was devastated." As was Adriana, I could see it in her mannerisms. Moira and Granny must have been close, and her following words backed that up, "We always had a good visit, did Moira and me."

I watched the ghostly visitor as Adriana spoke and noted she listened with interest but without any other emotions. It was as if she heard a sad tale that had nothing to do with herself. Then she looked over to me and winked when she caught me watching. How odd.

"Was she a Shadow Dancer?" I asked.

"Yes. A strong one too. We all had such hopes Moira would be able to track all three of them, bringing Jessica, Addy, and Charlie home." My great-grandmother sighed then changed the subject back to the matter at hand. "Now, how are we going to tackle this going forward? We have to get to the book from the forbidden library and find the spell. We need to find out why Harley was killed or suicided, although I'm leaning toward murder—it is too coincidental that he had information for us then killed himself before telling us what it was. Who would do that? No. This is murder. We have to see if they are linked and get to Donna. She has the answers. It's quite the list of things to accomplish."

"Edith told me she'd been on the lower levels twice. What has she told you?" I looked over to Edith, who was hovering behind Jake and Becky, and raised my brows at her, asking her the silent question even as I mentioned it to Adriana.

"Fine! I'm only wanted around here when you decide you need me." Edith sniffed, looking dejected, and floated around to stand by the fireplace.

"Why don't you tell us what you know, Edith. I can put a spell on some paper so as you speak, everyone else can read along and know what you are saying. Please?" I could be polite.

"What? She's still here?" Jake asked, peering around warily. Becky pulled the pillow off her face and sat up.

"Why can't all witches see and hear ghosts? If they are out there and we live in the paranormal, how come only some witches...very, very few at that, can see or hear them?" she asked.

"I'm not sure about that one, dear. I know it's rare and useful. In this case, anyway. Many witches don't advertise they have the ability for obvious reasons. Too many loved ones wanting answers to questions, too many folks don't like the idea of a ghost hanging around watching them," proclaimed Adriana sagely. It made sense in a way. I know I didn't like having to wonder if I had a ghostly observer every time I prepared to shower!

Reaching for my notebook, I tore out three pages and placed one each in front of Andrea, Jake and Becky, then I called up my magic and chanted a copy spell that would have whatever Edith said become words on the pages my friends could follow along. A handy trick and one I'd eagerly learned from Adriana. She was nodding in approval at my crafting abilities. Finally, I opened my notebook to a fresh page and looked expectantly at Edith, ready to take notes. "OK, you have the floor, um, so to speak. Tell me what you know."

Edith's demeanor brightened considerably, and she hastened to tell her tale. "Well, you see. I had received a special assignment from one of the Council Elders."

Andrea, Jake, and Becky's eyes widened as the words appeared in delicate cursive across the lines of the page. Edith continued, "I was to go down to the lowest level of the library and get a very ancient and dark spell that was in one of the tomes for this person. On my first attempt, I managed to get past the Sentinels because this Elder gave me a specific draught that would make them ignore me." Adriana sat up straight at this revelation, appearing shocked.

"I failed to find the spell, however. When I returned, the Elder gave me another task. Find if a previous witch had left behind any trace magic because that book should never have been removed from the forbidden library—could not, in fact, and was insistent that it had to be there still. When I returned the second time, halfway through my task, the draught stopped working, and the Sentinels awakened."

We all gasped in shock and Andrea asked Edith how she managed to escape.

"I almost didn't. I hid in a cupboard in an odd room that had all manner of weird objects in it. Many things I'd never seen before in my life, and I couldn't even begin to describe. I could hear the Sentinels coming for me, but then I reached into my pocket, and my fingers happened to touch a small figurine, a smooth stone animal totem, that the Elder had given me. The Sentinels began to moan, then stopped looking for me altogether."

Edith paused, then drifted over to the fireplace and stared at the flames a moment before completing her tale. "I held the totem in my fist and managed to reach the door to the upper levels, but I couldn't proceed. Something was blocking me from escape. When I realized it might be the wee familiar I was holding, I dropped it, able to cross to the upper level, where I fled up the stairs to safety. Even as I dropped it, I could hear the Sentinels shift from unaware to super-focused on my whereabouts. I can still hear their frustrated gnashing and snarling complaints at my escape. It's something I don't think I will ever forget."

"Who sent you down there, Edith? And did you ever find

the traces of magic to identify who took the dark spell?" Adriana asked with trepidation and interest.

Edith gazed at Adriana and looked ashamed. What on earth could she be about to tell us that had her worried so?

"Oh, all right. I am in this far, and it's not like you can punish me for what I've concealed all this time."

Now I was definitely curious and a bit apprehensive myself. I tried to remain calm even as Edith's following words registered.

"Olivia. Olivia Ogden-Meyers sent me to find out if the Book of Ancients had been tampered with and the spell removed. Not only had the book been opened, but it looked as if someone had ripped out a small section, the passage removed, and I know who took them and why." Edith looked sadly at me and then down at her hands, nervously fiddling with the hem of her shirt.

"Tell us, Edith. What did you find?" I asked, gently.

"I found traces of magic that left a residue on the remaining tome. I collected that residue and brought it to Olivia. When she tested the magic, she realized she needed to make a truth serum to have whoever cast the spell reveal all. She didn't need the person who cast it; she used me as a surrogate instead. When she had me drink the potion that she made from the remnant filtrate, then asked me to divulge my secrets, I opened my mouth and told her not only who stole the passages but when and why. It was Deanna Fredricks. She took them to create the magic that turned Adelaide and caused Charles to forget Sweet Briar and his family. It was the very magic you need to look for, but it's gone now. Without those passages, you have nothing."

You could have heard the proverbial pin drop in that room. Except for the fire crackling in the hearth, no one made a sound; we were so astounded.

"Oh, Edith. All this time, you knew?"

"Are you certain someone took the reversal spell? Or just the one to cast the first curse on Adelaide and the next on Charlie?" Adriana queried.

"The passage you need to reverse the spell is down there still, locked away in a glass dome. And only a certain type of magic can find it. But I am not sure what that is. Olivia might, however," said Edith.

I was furious with this news. "Olivia! I thought she was an ally. Why would she keep this information from us?" I cried.

Olivia was a Veritum—the highest form of Seeker, someone who went after the truth at all costs, like a tenacious terrier. She was just like her grand-nephew Brian Chase in that regard. Yes, *that* Brian Chase.

Adriana had such a gloomy deportment that I almost felt sorry for Olivia when she tracked her down, seeking those same answers.

"That's what I'd like to know, Liliana. That is what I most certainly would like to know."

CHAPTER 9

*M*y patience with Lorcan was running thin, as I found myself out and about a couple of days later with Jake and Andrea in tow. Our usual foursome had grown by one with the addition of Becky to our mix, but now that she had to be at her bookshop, and Lorcan was still pouting in his garage, we were down to three dedicated sleuths.

I get that we are amateurs. I comprehend that when you look into every murder or mystery that I've stumbled upon, it was usually a series of unfortunate events that brought the baddy to justice. Or some other much better amateur sleuth managed to save the day. I get it. My track record is sketchy at best. That wouldn't stop my enthusiastic pursuit of whoever did poor Harley Jacobs in. And we are talking about murder.

The preliminary police findings verified that the tiny potion vial contained a poison, an herbal concoction made out of yellow jessamine, a prolific vine here in the South, also known as Carolina jasmine. A tincture of which could paralyze a grown man in a matter of minutes. Kill one with a large enough portion. The ruling was still out, but it was presumed a murder over suicide because someone left the bottle on the victim's chest.

Since no one could figure out why Harley would be chugging jessamine, it seems murder would be an intelligent assumption. That and the video footage from the Murphy's motel showed a grainy passenger in the front seat of Harley's truck as he drove by, then after pulling into the gas station, another shadowy figure running away from the business and into the woods on the opposite side of the street. Brian had stated it wasn't the best surveillance equipment, so identifying who this mystery figure was would be virtually impossible.

I was grateful that Brian had consented to share even that much with us, well, Jake anyway.

Today, we were meeting Adriana at her request, although none of us knew her plans. I'd wondered if she had confronted Olivia yet, but I knew she'd let us know in good time.

"Did you try calling him?" Andrea, ever the worrier, was convinced that one phone call would set things straight between Lorcan and me. She underestimated my stubbornness, however.

"Andrea. Why should I call him? To say what? That I'm sorry? I am not even remotely sorry because I did nothing wrong. If Lorcan wants to assume the worst about me, then maybe we shouldn't go any further with whatever the heck it is we have been doing."

Jake cleared his throat and stuck up for his friend. Imagine that. "Uh, I hate to point this out, especially in light of how upset you are right now, but weren't you the one who tossed him out of your place the other day and not give him a chance to explain the Nora situation?"

He had a point.

Sigh. I hate when that happens.

Although Jake should talk, especially since he and Lorcan had a tenuous relationship because of dear Nora, another long story.

"Well, I have to stop in and grab those packages to be mailed to my online customers. If he is at the shop and wants to talk, I can manage a minute or two."

I could see the eye-rolls even though I wasn't looking at either one of my friends, but I chose to refrain from any more commentary and marched in the direction of Found Things, my art studio. I could hear Lorcan barking orders to Stu and Jack even before I reached the alley that separated our two places of business. It sounded like someone was in a foul mood. Good. I hoped he was miserable. Well, I could match his mood and raise it ten bucks.

Lifting the warehouse door, I continued my march into the studio and over to the shelving that held the labeled boxes ready for post. Jake and Andrea followed, and in an unusually high-pitched squeak, I heard Andrea greet Lorcan a few moments later.

"Lorcan! Hi there. How are you? We missed you the other night at, um. How're things?" She added lamely. Nice one, there, Dre. Real smooth.

"Hey man, can you stop acting like a jerk and swallow your pride and talk to your girlfriend, please? She is just as much of an asshat as you are, and Andrea can't take much more angst." Leave it to Jake, the attorney, to cut to the chase.

I turned and found Lorcan glaring at me, ignoring Jake and Andrea and holding a rather large wrench in his hand. I mean massive, like as tall as a child massive. It looked like it could do serious damage to someone should they get conked on the head with it.

"Is that for me? Do you intend to whack me on my

noggin? Am I supposed to go run screaming, so you'd give chase?"

Lorcan looked confused for a minute, but then realization dawned, and his frown returned.

"Do you want to tell me why it is perfectly fine for you to pitch a hissy fit about an error of omission on my part to remove an insignificant banns of marriage from the Council? Especially when you expect me to be cheery and pleasant after finding your face pressed up against your ex-boyfriend? And I'm sure it wasn't because you were giving him mouth to mouth for survival purposes. You were nowhere near Nichols Pond this time, so you don't even have that as an excuse."

He jests.

I was not amused.

"Not until you explain to me how you could think registering for marriage to a skank that tried to shoot both of us with a fake gun and played a key role in corrupting several youths in this town is insignificant. I wonder how many future wives you have registered? Maybe this is something you often do. Should we take a vote as to how many women you have in your holding pen? Do you frequently date skanks?"

I rounded my stance, facing Lorcan head-on, with my hands on my hips and a scowl to beat all scowls on my face.

"I don't know. Not unless you've been keeping that from me. Is that typed out on your résumé as a formerly held position?"

"Oh man, you didn't," groaned Jake, as Andrea gasped and backed away from the two of us.

My eyes went to slits, and I could feel my fingers twitching with magic.

"Take that back."

"Why should I?"

"Take that back, Lorcan."

"Why? You basically called me a man-slut. Or a philandering future polygamist. Or...or..."

"A philandering what?" I suddenly bent over and made horrible gasping sounds that wracked my entire body. Andrea, forgetting her fear, came rushing over to see if I was ill or spelled. Even Jake reached out to steady me, only to jump back in alarm when I straightened, throwing my head back. I was laughing so hard it deteriorated into a series of hiccups worse than those that had afflicted me the other day at the gas station.

"A philandering, future...poly...hah! Oh, my gosh...man-slut!" I was wheezing at this point, and when I fixed my eyes to Lorcan's, I could see he was struggling to keep his lips from twitching with mirth. His eyes, however, were sparkling even though his frown was still in place.

He walked over to me and shook me by the shoulders, so my head rattled, then planted a big wet kiss on my lips, growling a little as he did.

"Don't ever let that man kiss you again, or there will be another murder in this town. Do you understand?"

I nodded and managed to huff out, "Only if you promise not to put any more women on the register at the Tribunal...unless I approve of them first." He nodded yes, then laughed aloud, hugging me to his chest.

Lorcan agreed, then whispered in my ear, "I really like your new Jeep."

"You two are nuts." Jake walked over to a metal chair and took a seat, shaking his head back and forth. "Mental...both of you."

Andrea just looked weepy yet happy at the same time. I guessed she was grateful the tension had passed, and Lorcan and I were back on again. Poor Andrea.

"What are you three doing? No, wait. Let me guess. You have your investigative hats on again, right?"

I nodded then told him about our upcoming meeting with Adriana.

"What is she up to? Any ideas?"

"Wouldn't you like to know, you wanton Lothario?"

In waltzed my great-grandmother like she owned the place, and we were expecting her. We collectively jumped then gaped in awe when we contemplated her outfit. Adriana had a skin-tight turtleneck and legging ensemble on, all black. She had woven a long, knitted scarf around her neck, in a midnight blue, with moons and stars and a few planets embossed on it in silver threading. The combat boots on her feet made her height go up by two entire inches and would have given her the guise as an aged French spy if it weren't for her hat choice.

She sported a pom-pom hat on top of her head. It was so inharmonious with the rest of her outfit—it being bright green with the pom-poms a metallic orange—that she looked like a middle-schooler whose parents let them dress without checking to make sure it was presentable. On her tiny person, the outfit looked garish at best and obscene, especially when you considered just how tight those leggings were, at its worst. So much so we were rendered speechless.

"Like it, huh? I found it at Goodwill the other day."

"The hat? Or the entire outfit?"

"Hey! I paid fourteen dollars for the boots alone, thank you very much. It's my new winter detecting and reconnaissance garb. I can't go on a mission dressed in my usual clothing!"

Yes, because pointy hats and spiderweb shawls clashed with espionage so.

"But I don't understand, Granny." Andrea frowned and wrinkled her nose. "That doesn't even remotely look like a detective costume. If you showed up in a trench coat like Columbo or even a hat like Sherlock Holmes, well, then I'd get it. But a pom-pom hat?"

"I will have you know, some of the greatest minds in the business wear these types of hats."

"What business?" I asked, "Newspaper delivery?"

"Keep it up, dummy, and you will feel my wrath."

Now it was my turn to roll my eyes.

"Yeah, yeah...promises, promises. Why are you even here? I thought we were supposed to meet you at the Council in a few minutes. Why'd you come across town only to have to head back over now?"

"Because I've changed my mind. We aren't going to the Council. We are going to the prison instead."

Jake shot out of his seat like a cannon. "Hold on a second. You can't. The Council has a holding cell for when someone requests to see a prisoner at their facility. No one goes to the prison! No one I know has the exact location of the actual prison, anyway. It's a highly guarded secret. There is no way you could have found out where its location is."

"And yet I did."

Jake was sputtering and looked agog at my diminutive granny.

"But...but, how?"

"I slept with the Head of Security. Now let's go. Andiamo! Pronto!"

Gah!

* * *

"You could have told us Grandpa Antonio used to be on the Board of Directors for the prison and held the title Head of Security before scarring us for life, you know," I grumbled as Adriana chortled behind me in the backseat of my new Jeep.

"Why? I liked the way your faces collectively blanched the way they did. You looked paler then Edith on a good day." Shoulders rocking, my great-grandmother surveyed her surroundings in my vehicle. "I like this one way better than the one you used to have, Andrea. Although I still can't believe you got rid of it for that tiny wagon of yours."

"Hey. Subaru Outback's are very reliable cars."

"Yeah, but this fun baby could run over your itty-bitty wagon and flatten you like a pancake. I like being up this high. Maybe I should get one of these things, too."

Eek.

Considering Granny, at one hundred or so, still tore around town in a giant Lincoln Town Car, terrorizing the citizens of Sweet Briar with her driving acumen—or lack thereof, I didn't think it wise that she was considering something that was four-wheel drive. And it could climb the sides of mountains with ease.

"I like to hike and thought I'd take up mountain climbing or spelunking. A Jeep could be useful. Think of all the off-roading I could do."

Case in point.

I informed Adriana just how much I paid for this fun baby and noticed that she blanched a spectral white as well. I think she'll be sticking with her Lincoln for the foreseeable future. It wasn't that she didn't have the money, far from it, my grandparents were loaded. However, Granny was a tad on the cheap side with some things, and cars fell into that category.

Andrea was sitting in front with me while Jake and Lorcan followed behind in Jake's Mercedes. Lorcan decided to leave the shop in the good hands of his two employees and tag along to: "keep you lot out of trouble."

Little did he know, trouble was fast becoming my middle name. As for Adriana? They invented the word after she was born, I'm sure.

"Hang on a minute. Isn't that Susanne's church? And if that's true, oh, wow. Please tell me we aren't heading into the abandoned cabin rental place that Donna owned. Why are we turning into the parking lot? How could you do this to me?"

Donna and her despicable son, Beau "Bubba" Buford, had kidnapped me when I first arrived in town and held me prisoner for a bit at one of the derelict cabins. An ordeal I would genuinely love to forget. That Granny was heading into the parking area now had me shaking, not with residual fear, but with anger that I was fooled by those two, as was my mother, Aunt Jessica. Um...yeah. I will get there someday.

"No, the entrance isn't here. And no, it isn't in the church because, as you well know, that is the main entrance to the forbidden area of the library. We are meeting someone here who has the key to the secret entrance into the jail."

Secret, what? Why did this suddenly feel like an Austin Powers flick?

"Who, or wait...why are we risking so much to sneak into the prison? We have enough evidence to present to the Council and request aid. Maybe they can locate Donna faster than..."

"Request? Evidence! Cara, do you expect me to divulge what we've discovered about Adelaide to those bumbling idiots? *Stupida!* Do you want them to come and take your cat, wrenching Addy out of her? Don't you suppose it might mean lights out for the kitty part of that equation?"

Perhaps the Council wouldn't be concerned about one black cat, magical or not. But now that Adriana mentioned it, it would be prudent to hold all our cards close. What if whatever spells they used to free Adelaide took them both out?

Jeebers!

Of course, after pondering the revelation that Adelaide merged with my cat Wicked, I'd lain awake nights wondering what would happen if we successfully freed Adelaide and saved Wicked as well. Would Wicked suddenly lose her magical awareness? Even worse, would she age to the twenty-year-old cat she was, then wither away, decrepit, and ripened into a very typical old cat?

What would Adelaide be like after living the last twenty odd years part of a feline surrogate?

I reached in my cup holder and grabbed a handful of black jellybeans. I ate them like candy when I was nervous. Um...right.

Lorcan and Jake pulled alongside us. I opened my window, and Lorcan did the same as a figure showed up, walking out of the camp and over to our vehicles.

"Is that Old Frank?"

It was. A hermit of sorts and estranged brother to Abner, the handyman who keeps showing up at my home without an invitation, Old Frank usually could be found in the woods wandering the area and tending his many purported moonshine stills. His pack of dogs as his only companions, I found Frank harmless.

I met Old Frank a few weeks back when I was dealing with the murder of Edith and the crazed and possessed teen, Rowan Nightingale. Throw Nora and Lorcan in the mix, along with that wretched Maureen Kennedy and her pimple-faced beau, Tommy, and we had quite the party going. That is until a storm knocked me out of commission. OK, fine. I managed to knock myself out in the brouhaha with a magical spell gone awry and wound up at Old Frank's cabin. There I remained until the storm raging outside ceased and Brian Chase had time to clean up the mess I'd left in my wake.

"Morning, Frank," Lorcan called out to the approaching man.

"Yep."

Frank was a man of few words.

We scrambled out of our vehicles and walked over to where he waited with his dog pack.

"Let me have that key, and you can be on your way, Frank," Adriana commanded, holding her hand out for the item in question.

"Can't give it."

Waves of odiferous moonshine poured off the man, and I wondered if he was drunk, although his eyes were clear—and he seemed steady on his feet.

Appearing shocked then perturbed at being thwarted by the mountain man, Adriana arched an eyebrow and demanded to know why.

"You said you had it safe. Why can't you give it to me now? Did you lose it?"

"No."

Exasperated at this point, Adriana glared at the man, who didn't so much as quake at her ire.

"Then why won't you hand it over?"

"Rusty."

We eyeballed one another, wondering how long Old Frank had to live before my great-grandmother let loose a firestorm of magic, smiting the hapless man into a pile of ashen boozy dust.

"Who is Rusty, and why does that man have the key?"

"Rusty ain't no man. That be Rusty, there."

Pointing to a rather shaggy wolf-like dog, all shades of brown and rust and black, with a large set of shining white teeth on full display as his tongue lolled out between pants, we tracked our eyes over to Adriana to see what she'd say next.

"How on earth can a dog have that key? It's not like he can hold it without having thumbs! What do you mean he has the key? Is it around his neck? Does he bite or something?"

Old Frank sighed, shaking his head woefully at the massive beast, then turned once more to Adriana and explained.

"You see. Ol' Rusty, he's a bit of a prankster. And as I was a reachin' to take the key down off the hook, well he done jumped up and swallowed it in one gulp. I walked him, and I walked him. Fed him some rabbit. I even gave him a bit of my coffee. Nothing. Now we jest have to wait on Rusty and have nature take its course before we see that key agin!"

The way my great-grandmother was looking at Rusty, I wouldn't take bets we'd have to wait all that long.

Run, Rusty. Run!

CHAPTER 10

"Well, that was educational."

Who knew you could extract anal glands making a dog poop well before it had planned on doing so? See what I missed not having a pet all these years due to my Aunt Jessica's aversion to, no, wait...hey! I got it correct this time! Aunt Jessica!

What was I saying?

We were back in our vehicles and headed to the secret location, which would lead us to the back entrance of the prison. I know! It sounds like I've fallen into a bad James Bond movie. Only we didn't have cool gadgets and weapons—but *were* the weapons! The thing that worried me was knowing the guards inside most assuredly had magic at their disposal. So, it wasn't like we would be the force to be reckoned with—there would be a reckoning on both sides.

We went another few miles up the road then parked in a nondescript area of gravel and weeds. As we began trudging along a path near a rustic-looking stone bridge, I realized we were dancing relatively close to the North Carolina border. I couldn't help but find my mind wandering to my new ghost problem as we wound our way down the trail.

Why was I hesitating to tell Adriana that Moira Muir Fortune had shown up and was seemingly happy to impart kindly words of wisdom and manipulate my table settings? Was it because I feared she'd freak out when the realization I could see and hear her old friend and that she could not? I knew I'd have to sit down with Granny sooner rather than later and go over all these unanswered questions and start connecting the dots to make a pattern. Maybe then we'd have all the answers and could solve these puzzles.

I just wish we didn't have so many of them!

Those musings would have to wait as we came upon a meandering stream that led to a rusted but solid-looking gate. By the gate, I meant door-sized, prison bar thick, and sporting a chain and lock straight out of the Dark Ages. It was ancient and unwieldy.

"I know I've only been aware of my powers for a few short months, but unless I'm mistaken, that gate is oozing magic, and I'm assuming that means it's heavily warded." I probed.

Adriana was already nodding her head, yes, and rubbed her chin as she eyed the imposing piece of metal and magic. Lorcan and Jake kept turning their heads this way and that, seeming to be on some kind of guard duty, but all it was managing to do was make me distracted and irritable.

"Why do you keep peering around like you're waiting for a guy with a chainsaw to show up?"

"Sentinels." Lorcan all but whispered.

The hair on my neck and arms stood up as I shivered.

"They could be anywhere at this point since we are at this supposed back entrance. Although why a high-security dungeon would even have a back door to escape is beyond me. Talk about security risk," muttered Jake.

Andrea began scratching her elbow in a nervous tick, something she always denies doing. "Um...are they big? What do they look like? Do they eat people? Do they eat witches?"

With every question, Andrea's voice was getting shriller. I worried that at any moment, she would turn and run off like a startled gazelle on the African veldt. Only she'd not escape because these Sentinels would be the lions in hiding and take out the fool that left the herd in a panic, making for a prime target.

"Steady, pipsqueak. Sentinels are only inside warded places underground. They can't survive on the surface. It's how the Elders wished them created," Adriana informed us, "I've got this. Aspetta...wait."

Adriana tried to assure my quivering cousin and held her hand out to her in what I thought was an act of comfort. Instead, she made an open palm impatient gesture asking for one of the hoop earrings Andrea wore. Andrea consented, hurriedly removing one of the two she displayed in one ear. The other ear only held one earring—that was about as wild as her look got. "They aren't familial items, right?" asked Adriana, "good. But they are silver? Ah! Even better. I just need the one."

Granny walked over to the gate, stopping about five feet from it. We crowded around behind her, still spooked with the thought of the guardians despite being reassured.

"OK... here's the thing. I need one of you to take this key and stick it into the keyhole, then turn it once, clockwise. No more. Just one turn. Who's volunteering?"

We regarded the woman like she was daft.

"Why don't *you* do it?" Lorcan inquired, gazing at my great-grandmother with suspicion.

"Because I am old and feeble, and my eyesight isn't so good anymore. I might trip and fall into the stream, which is frigid. I could catch a cold if that happens."

"You are only old and feeble when it benefits you, old woman. What gives?" I sassed angrily.

"Am I not old?"

"Yes."

"Aren't old people feeble?"

"Yes, but you just *told* me you intend to take up mountain-climbing or spelunking, whatever the heck that is."

"Cave diving."

Now we really began staring at her like she'd gone barmy and needed a straitjacket to contain all that unbridled enthusiasm.

"What do you think will happen when we turn the key?" Andrea asked in a voice so soft and filled with trepidation. I expected she'd faint dead away in another minute or two from the anxiety of it all.

"I don't expect anything to happen."

"Liar. OK...fine. Give it to me," I snarled, palming the offensive key and galumphing over to the postern. Eyeing the intimidating entry, I cautiously inserted the key, pausing to mentally remember which way clockwise turned—hey, I was a basket of nerves—and moved the key one turn to the right as instructed.

Other than a grinding click sound, nothing much happened. We all collectively released the breath we held—all except Adriana, who looked apathetic.

"Told you."

Adriana snorted with her superior attitude on full display. Convinced she had been holding her breath in as well, I smirked.

Adriana hefted the little circlet of silver as if she weighed it, gauging its heaviness, but then efficiently chucked it over to the gate where it sailed through the bars and landed with a faint ping.

At first, nothing happened.

Suddenly a loud whoosh sounded followed by a roar so deafening; I lost my hearing. It was almost the same sensation one would get underwater or if you were about to pass out. That's when the air around us exploded, and we flew to the ground. Not waiting to see what would happen next, Lorcan scrambled up, ran over to Adriana, and scooped her up while Jake grabbed Andrea and me by the wrists. We tore off into the woods, not stopping until we reached the bridge.

"Punth mm dwn, oo foo."

That's what it sounded like anyway. I suspected Adriana was asking Lorcan to let go of his death grip. Quicker on the uptake than the rest of us, Lorcan gently settled Adriana back on her feet once more.

"Fools! Why did you take off running? Now we have to go all the way back again!"

"Back? No way are we going back! That blast almost killed us!" Jake screeched in a voice exceedingly high for a man's timbre. It sounded like a little girl squealing! But who was I to judge? If I even remotely could speak, I'm sure I'd squeak as well.

"That explosion did not almost kill us. The only one who has any right to complain is Mortimer."

We again stood there, ogling my great-grandmother as if she'd finally gone off the rails, plummeting into the abyss of insanity.

"Mortimer?" Lorcan asked.

"Mortimer," Adriana replied with a sniff.

Sounding shrill but nevertheless finding my voice, I shrieked, "who the heck is Mortimer?"

"I, am Mortimer."

I'm not ashamed to say each and every one of us, except for Adriana, screamed, spinning around when we heard the voice coming from behind. I am also ashamed to say we all screamed again once we got a gander at who...or rather, *what* was speaking.

"Oh my gosh, what is that? What *is* that?" Andrea shrieked then ran behind Lorcan, using him as a shield. The sight of him bare-chested had obviously given her the impression he'd be the one physically strongest in our group. Although with Lurch showing up and a good two and a half feet taller than my boyfriend, I suspected that Lorcan would be toast in a hand-to-hand fight with this guy even without magic.

I say Lurch because he looked just like the old Adam's Family television show character, complete with the slanty eyes, dark piercing look, lofty stature, and a gravelly voice straight out of the grave. This dude was massive. His shoulders were broader than any linebacker I've ever beheld—and he wasn't even wearing shoulder pads!

Jake was sputtering but finally managed to whisper, "That's the biggest man I've ever seen in my life." More like a walking stone wall.

"That's no man." Adriana cackled, "hear that, Morty? A man. No. Allow me to introduce you to Mr. Mortimer Snodgrass. He's a vampire."

Thud!

Down went Andrea like a sack of potatoes. I wished I could join her in her fainting slumber, but for once, I managed not to black out.

Lucky me.

* * *

"You couldn't have warned us? You couldn't have told us we'd be waking up a slumbering giant. An antediluvian vampire that could probably suck the life out of everyone present, and you decided it would be prudent *not* to mention this little fact?"

"I don't know why you children are fretting. I'm the one with the hole burned in my forehead, after all." Mortimer objected.

OK, so he did have a rather nasty-looking smoldering crevice in his forehead from where the silver earring had made contact. But it wasn't like we were aware of what Adriana was up to. Although, I'm not sure if he'd be any better off, considering we probably would have run off and left her to face this creature alone once we did comprehend what her plans were!

"Stop complaining! He isn't even a full vampire, are you Mort? He's part shifter too."

I looked blankly at my great-grandmother, blinking repetitively.

"Oh! That's right—newbie to all this paranormal stuff. Morty here is mostly all vamp, but his momma was half shifter and half vamp. His father is the pure-blooded vampire and even more ancient than this big guy here appears. I knew the minute the Council denied us a visit with Donna, I'd have no choice but to awaken old Morty here, so we could get in and get the job done."

Mortimer looked insulted at being called a vamp, and I nervously smiled at him, widening my eyes as if to say, ignore her. She's feebleminded. *Please* don't suck my blood.

"May I ask what a shifter is without sounding like an idiot?" I ventured into a question since I had no clue what anyone was talking about at this point.

Adriana snorted, so I leveled a look at her and pointed my index finger at her nose. "Don't trifle with me, old woman. I am not in the mood. Is it like, a werewolf or something?" I mentally went over all the movies I had watched and the few fantasy books I'd read and thought I made a relatively reasonable assumption—until everyone started giggling.

OK for my friends and family, but unnerving when

Mortimer did so as well. It sounded as if someone had just slid the lid of a sarcophagus open.

"No, Lily." Andrea explained, "A shifter is someone who can transform themselves into another being or inanimate object. One could mimic a wolf or any other animal if they felt like it, but most shifters choose to imitate people. They can doppelgänger someone with ease. Though some do have totem animals they are bonded with."

"Oh! I'm glad to know there aren't such things as were-wolves...vamp...um...we are all the paranormal I can handle," I finished lamely.

Mortimer smiled benignly at me in understanding. At least I think he did. His face transformed into every night-mare I'd ever had, and I couldn't be sure he wasn't sizing me up for a tasty snack.

"Who said there isn't any such thing as werewolves? I just said shifters aren't werewolves. Keep with the program, dummy," said Adriana.

Gulp.

"Now. Morty here has been enjoying his vacation going on; what has it been, dear? Sixty years? He has been kind enough to stand guard at the entrance your great-grandfa-ther constructed when heading security at this prison. Antonio added two Sentinels and a vampire. Mortimer's dad used to be the guard here before that, but he's in Boca now. Retired." Adriana beamed at us and patted Morty on the back, or behind. He was *really* tall.

Then Adriana's words registered. A vampire. Retiring to Boca Raton? All that sun? Huh.

"Isn't that, um...sun and surf and being a..." I didn't know where I was going here. My preconceived ideas had already gotten me ridiculed, so I was careful with what I said.

"Only the younglings burn to a crisp. Ancient vampires have discovered ways of protecting themselves from the sun, and most wear sunglasses day and night. It's not too bad." Adriana claimed. "Plus, Fred and Linda have a great condo...right on Lake Boca with a small marina for their boat. I had a great visit about fifty years ago now, lovely people, Morty's parents."

Fred and Linda?

"Wait! So, Mr. Snodgrass..."

"Mortimer, please."

"Uh...Mortimer, you're the Sentinel? Since my Granny stated you were the guardian of this gate."

Adriana frowned at me like I'm a student one comment away from getting sent to the corner and having to don a dunce cap.

"Of course, he isn't a Sentinel. And he wasn't guarding the gate. Aren't you paying attention yet? He *was* the gate. Well, the shield around it. No one or nothing would be able to get through it. Not with this big guy in the way. To anyone running amok in the twisted corridors of the prison, all they'd see would be another stone wall, seemingly impervious and thick. But the exit was there all this time. All you had to do was awaken Morty with a bit of silver."

"A bit? It will take me hours to regenerate my flesh, woman."

"You'll live." My great-grandmother's eyes flew open, and she threw her head back, barking out a huge laugh, "live...you...live. Get it? Oh, I crack myself up sometimes."

Mortimer was *not* amused. Neither were we.

"So, what do we do now?" asked Jake. He was giving Mortimer a wide berth and was still rather pale.

"Now we go into the prison and try to find out where Donna has been keeping herself and strangle the information we need out of her miserable hide."

Mortimer looked solemnly at Adriana, his face a mask of regret.

"I'm afraid that will not be possible, my dear."

It was Adriana's turn to looked nonplussed, then flustered.

"Why on earth not? Don't start spouting rules at me, Morty. We made those rules when we funded that prison, or my Antonio's family, anyway. Why do you think he had that secret entrance put there? It has aided many a Dolce on both sides of the law."

I bet.

"Annie, dear. It is not that I forbid this. It's that I cannot allow it. The lowest level of the prison has become unstable. A renegade witch has indeed found her way down there. But instead of being ripped to shreds by the depraved, wasting away for centuries, this evil woman turned them into an army. A small one, but a dedicated and cagey one, none-theless, if rumors are true. The Council has been keeping a lid on this, which is probably why they refused to allow an audience. Why...if I had to guess," he stated in his primordial and resonating voice, "the very witch who has become a Queen of the Damned down there is more than likely the same as the one you are trying to find!"

Oh, you *think* so, buddy?

Somehow, I didn't believe this news would be met with acceptance by my demonic great-grandmother. I wasn't disappointed. After all, she infers she's taught Old Beelzebub a few tricks. I doubt she'd play second fiddle to one Donna Fredericks.

This was going to end in war. I just knew it.

"We'll just see about that! If I have to tear this prison down to the foundations to get that witch, I will."

Yep...war.

CHAPTER 11

*E*arly the following day, I found myself standing in a barnyard looking at a charming if a tad neglected farmhouse. Andrea and I came to pay our respects to the Jacobs, Harley's parents. I wasn't looking forward to this, but I felt it only fitting to bring a casserole and our sympathies. The South and its traditions were undoubtedly rubbing off on me!

The door opened before we reached the porch, and a sad-looking woman with kindly eyes met us at the top step.

"Andrea, dear. And this must be the long, lost, Lily Sweet. Please, won't you come in? Oh, and a casserole, too. Aren't you just dears?"

We followed Mrs. Jacobs into her home and noted how lonely the place felt. There would never be any grandchildren or great-grandchildren running around the house, not hers anyway. I placed her at about eighty years old, and the man sitting at the kitchen table, where she led us, looked to be a couple of years older than his wife. Mr. Jacobs, I presume. Although Andrea informed me, they were only in their late sixties—farming must be hard work.

"Aren't these lovely ladies just so charitable to stop in and see how we are doing, dear?"

The older man barely smiled but nodded his head in our direction.

"No one to help with the farm now. Going to sell it all and move to a retirement home."

What do you say to that? Andrea gave me a worried look and walked around to the man, reaching her hands out and grasping his outreaching ones.

"I'm so sorry. I can't imagine how much pain you must be feeling. Harley was a good man. Lily and I want you to know we are going to do everything in our power to find out what happened and bring you some closure."

I was nodding yes but quaked at the weight of responsibility Andrea just put on our shoulders. It was one thing to say in private that you planned on catching a murderer, quite another, however, to promise this to the grieving parents of the man!

"I can tell you what happened. Deanna Fredricks. That's what happened. If my son had never gotten involved with that hussy, that...that...witch. Oh! I'm sorry. I know you all aren't like that woman. It's just..." Mrs. Jacobs sat down at the table, placing her palms down and leaning toward us, her voice subdued once more. "That Deanna and her sister Donna, they were eviler than anyone in Sweet Briar was aware. I don't know what Harley needed to tell you, Lily. But I do know he'd found some old papers; love notes and photos and such. He must have discovered something that triggered a memory or whatnot. After all, he came in here talking blazes about setting things to right and telling your Adriana what went down all those years back when your momma ran off with you."

I didn't bother correcting her about Jessica and Adelaide. The less who knew right now, the better.

"I have this box here for you." Mr. Jacobs informed us. "I was saving it, waiting until the right time. But seeing as you are here..."

Mr. Jacobs got up from his seat and took a medium-sized box off a shelf in the open pantry. It was worn and had a moldy smell like someone stored it in a garage, basement...or barn.

"I don't know what you'll find in there. Don't matter much to me. Just find out who killed my boy. Please get my boy some justice."

We agreed.

"He started dating after all these years. Did you know that? Not that we are upset. We were thrilled for him. He's was only in his early forties. His girlfriend lives down in Tiger, and her parents have a farm as well. She is only thirty-five. I don't think the age difference mattered to them. I had to call the poor dear and let her know about my Harley. Oh! Listen to me going on. You have better things to do than listen to an old woman's troubles. Just find out what happened, please."

Again, we agreed then left shortly after that.

I was quiet on the drive back to town, and I knew it was time to brainstorm. We needed a plan. I was exhausted, and I guessed Andrea was likely to be as worn out as I felt.

Vampire. Shape-shifting ones! Who knew Mortimer favored shifting into walls of stone as his idea of a grand vacation. More like the side of a mountain. And sleeping for sixty years? Who did that? Vampires, I supposed. Werewolves or no werewolves, and shifters and, who knows what else!

Donna amassing an army of heaven-knows-what, and my dad out there embroiled in whatever mischief the Romano clan of the Pacific Northwest was cooking up, had me worried. I had so many thoughts rattling around my head—Harley's murder. Me still needing to get into the forbidden level of the darned library and find the reversal spell to free my mom—even though Edith insisted Deanna Fredricks locked them away. Adriana convinced Edith couldn't have removed the spells from the forbidden section if she wanted to. Freeing both Adelaide and Wicked--Is it any wonder I was nursing a migraine to beat all migraines?

Don't even get me started on my ghost problem.

This morning I'd found Edith staring daggers at my Great Aunt Moira, who was steadfastly ignoring the younger specter and continuing to knit like she didn't have a care in the world. Who knew? Maybe she didn't. I mean, how hard could being a spook be?

Before we parted yesterday after our disastrous day trip, I managed to corner Adriana and inform her she and I needed a private moment to go over some things that had come up. She looked intrigued but also suspicious, and I think she realized I had been withholding information from her. I was not looking forward to our meeting tonight.

Confronting Edith did me no good. She refused to speak to me again. Moira was no better, wishing me a "guid day. I didnae have much planned, and ye don't have tae worry aboot entertaining me! I'll be enjoying the sunlight. It leaves me right cadgy; it does! Don't know about herself over there. She's a bit dwaumie if ye ken what I mean."

More words to look up.

I'd be a polyglot in no time.

I'd left them to it, and now I was worried about what I'd find upon returning home. Wicked, certainly seemed put out by our resident ghosts. She had taken quite an instant dislike to Edith after seemingly adoring her when she had first manifested into my life. Now, however, every time Edith popped in, Wicked would poof up like I'd tossed her in the dryer, forgetting to use fabric softener sheets. It wasn't a pretty sight.

Just before I'd left today, Wicked was strutting back and forth in the kitchen, stiff-legged and irate, her tail lashing back and forth, letting anyone and everyone know she did not appreciate sharing her home with Edith. Maybe it had to do with Edith's foul mood. I didn't know because no one was talking to me. So—shrugging in a, I am Switzerland, totally staying neutral, thanks, way—I had bid them adieu and high-tailed it out of there. I crossed my fingers on the way out and sent a prayer up to the heavens that I'd find my place intact upon returning.

"Where to next?" Bringing me out of my reverie, Andrea brought up a good question. I had no idea where to even begin with our investigation.

The air had warmed slightly from this morning, and I could sense Spring quietly making a move in our direction. I cracked the window of my Jeep open and breathed in the fresh air with a promise of things to come. Flowery things.

"Why don't we go speak with Donald and Doreen? They were outside painting all day. I'm sure Brian has already gone over everything to go over with them, but you never know what they might be able to tell us. Brian certainly won't be sharing with me. I don't think." Best to leave that alone and not go seeking any aid, lest Lorcan have a conniption. Quite frankly, if Brian wouldn't respect that we were no longer an item, I needed to keep my distance, anyway.

"Good idea. I haven't seen the Murphys since the Christmas Eve party on the square!" Andrea stated.

Heading in the direction of Sweet Briar, Georgia's only motel, I began wondering if we were biting off more than we could chew. After all, if the police didn't have any leads. The gossip mill in town hadn't figured out any and spread them hither and yon yet. How could my gaggle of amateur sleuths and I find any?

I shuddered slightly as we passed the gas station where I'd

found Harley Jacobs only four days ago. It seemed like ages; so much had happened since then. I knew the police had released his body, and the Jacobs family were having a small private ceremony on Saturday and would bury their only child. I felt so badly for them.

As I approached the motel, I noticed that both Donald and Doreen were still working in their side yard. It looked like they'd finished painting the shutters and trim but now were gardening. In February? Oh, right. Donald did mention his peas and such going in before the end of the week. I couldn't even remember what I had done with mine ever since Wicked swiped them onto the kitchen floor. Maybe she ate them. Ah! Bowl, on the counter. I never did get the little tiller, however.

Sigh.

Hopping out of my Jeep, I beamed at my two elderly friends and paused to take in the fresh paint and new window boxes that adorned the front of the motel. "Looking good, you two. This place is downright homey!"

"That's the idea. We aren't any old run-down motel. Our place is clean and safe, and now it's spruced up, ready for Springtime and festival season to start up again!" Doreen beamed at me.

"Did ya plant them peas I gave you, Lily?" Donald asked. I murmured something and tried to look nonchalant. Thankfully he took it as a yes, and I crossed my fingers behind my back and promised myself I'd stop in at Ace Hardware since Dennis Carter didn't carry any tillers at his shop and get set up with all the proper tools I'd need to put in a little garden plot.

"You've got a lovely garden going in, Donald." Andrea maintained. "What are you planting now?"

"Beans. Early crop. Only these won't grow so big I'd have to worry 'bout no giants climbing down no vines." I laughed at his Jack and the Beanstalk reference, assured in the knowledge that giants, at least, were fictional.

I hoped.

"What can we do for you ladies?"

"We thought we'd ask around and maybe help the police find out anything more about what happened to poor Harley Jacobs," Andrea said.

"You mean you're investigating."

"Well...yes. I guess you could say that." I stated.

Donald looked at Doreen, who quietly handed him a one-dollar bill.

"Told you, woman. These two and their Granny can't keep their noses out of trouble. You owe me a steak dinner too."

I didn't know if I felt insulted with the realization folks were placing bets on my snooping ways or flattered that they expected me to do so.

"Come on inside, girls. I need to make a quick call, and then we can talk."

Seeing as Doreen was part of the Gossip Girls, I could guess she'd be spreading the word that I was on the case and for everyone to batten down the hatches, although I hadn't made any nefarious magic errors lately. But you never knew.

"Come in, come in. Have a seat. Let me get you some sweet tea...unless you'd like hot?" We didn't want to cause too much trouble, so we agreed to sweet tea, cold, with levels of sugar that made dentists around the world swoon in anticipation. It was the drink du jour in these parts, known as 'the house wine of the South.'

Donald shuffled in and ambled over to the sink, where he washed up. Then he opened the cabinet, took down a plastic rectangle storage container, and placed it on the table. "Mother made some of her butter cookies. I think you ladies would enjoy them with your beverage."

Mother? Oh...he must mean Doreen. I was still getting used to the lingo down here, although I believe I heard that used a time or two up in New York State with the older set.

Doreen bustled in and nodded her approval at Donald for providing us with treats, then took her seat and clasped her hands. "Now, what can we do that will help?"

"You can get the girls the tea you promised, woman!"

"Oh! Land sakes, where is my mind?" Doreen went to stand up, but Donald waved her back down, getting us the refreshments instead. When he completed that task, he took the seat opposite Doreen and patiently waited for us to begin.

"Well, we need to hear from both of you, just exactly what you observed on Sunday. Don't describe what you viewed on the surveillance tape...just try to remember the day and what you witnessed as it happened.

"That will be easy!" cried Doreen. "We saw Harley drive by, and the only reason we bothered to notice was the fact he was doing well over the speed limit as he flew by our place. I could feel the rumble of his truck and the wind he stirred up got dirt and dust all over the shutter I was painting! Donald had to wait for it to dry, then sand it all over again and repaint it the next day!"

"He was speeding? Harley?" I remembered the conversation we'd had that past Friday when he'd almost flattened me under his truck. Didn't he say he never sped...like ever? "Are you sure? I ask because Harley had just informed me that he never..."

"He never sped. He always obeyed the law to a fault. Didn't drink no more ever since his Deanna days, and after they'd broken up, he gave up the bottle and became a model citizen. Drove me nuts being stuck behind him a time or two. Worse than being trapped behind a school bus, it was!" Donald groused, then sobered when he realized he'd never have to worry about getting stuck behind Harley's truck ever again.

"What else do you remember? Detective Chase mentioned a passenger in the front with Harley. I don't suppose you could see anything that could help us?" Andrea asked.

"But that's just it!" cried Doreen, "I did see a person on the passenger side. I could swear it was one of them teenagers that got in trouble a few weeks back. One of the two boys that lit those firecrackers in the old playground right before those planes came flying overhead. Do you remember? The scavenger hunt and all?"

How could I forget?

"Do you mean one of the Kowalski Twins?" Andrea asked, and we looked shocked when she nodded yes.

"Have you informed Brian of this?"

Doreen looked a bit nervous, and I realized she must have omitted this tidbit from her report to Brian. But why?

"Doreen! You have to inform the police. They need to know this and..."

"And I figured you should be the one to maybe go speak with those boys and find out their excuse for being in Harley's truck right before he wound up dead. Murdered as it were. And if you get that information first, you might solve this case before the coppers."

Doreen looked proud at her declaration, and I couldn't fault her loyalty to me...just her timing. Brian needed that information to get justice for Harley and his parents, and I told her so.

"Now, Mother. I told you it looked like a gal in there. That weren't no teenage boy. Looked like a vagrant or hitch-hiker to me!" Donald stated.

"Well, you might be correct about that. I just know there

was someone in there, and even though Harley drove by but quick, I could tell he was upset."

"I sat there worrying my lip, wondering what to do with this information, if anything, when Doreen continued.

"Dead is dead, Lily. It's not like Harley would mind if it took a few extra days to solve his murder, right? As long as it is solved. So, why shouldn't it be you to have a leg up on the police and get to those boys before they do? If you hurry up, you can probably solve this case before the Jacobs bury their boy this Saturday."

Seeing as how this was Wednesday, I doubted very much the possibility of that happening.

* * *

DRIVING around town and looking for two young adult males who spent most of their free time causing mischief would not get us anywhere. So, Andrea and I did what any wise investigators would do. We went to Joe's Diner and had some lunch.

On our way over, Andrea confirmed with Steve Junior that the Kowalski boys had been away with their hapless mother, yet again, and could not have been our culprits...not that I thought Doreen had given us a solid lead, anyway.

We had to pass by the ill-fated gas station once more, not to mention Deputy Delaney's rental home. As we were driving by, we noticed Nora standing by her car. I don't know if she sensed my presence or not, but she suddenly looked up, and we made eye contact. Her eyes widened—and I don't think it was because I was riding high in my brand-new Jeep—but more the, I didn't expect to look up and see THAT witch gazing back at me, kind of moment.

The thing is, I had the overwhelming feeling she want-ed...no, needed to speak to me. Maybe it was the way she'd half-raised her hand like she wanted to flag me down, then dropped it suddenly, as if she thought better of that idea. What's with her? I turned to see if Andrea had noticed the odd occurrence, but she was going through her phone and didn't seem to be paying attention to her surroundings. And why would she? I was driving.

I would file Nora away for further consideration at a later date.

Walking into the diner, I wondered at how busy the place was for a weekday, that is until I noticed the chalkboard proclaiming Joe's special of the day—beef Wellington. Joe might own a diner and be the one and only chef, but he was a Cordon Bleu-trained chef of some standing. Every time I tasted another of his delectable offerings, I wondered that some restaurateur hadn't come calling and offered him a fancy position in a major city somewhere. Not that I'd ever think Joe would accept such a tantalizing offer. He loved this establishment and enjoyed being the boss.

Andrea and I waited for a booth to open up while sitting at the counter and nursing two colas. We didn't have to wait that long and rushed over to a table yet another new waitress bussed. This girl looked way too young to be the usual college student, let alone old enough to work. Looks could be deceiving, however.

She had just handed us our menus when a harried Sheila Polk came bustling over to us. "Thank you, Janelle. I've got these two ladies. Go refill the coffee."

Smiling, the girl wandered off, coffee pots in hand, decaf in the left and regular in the right, pouring and nodding to the patrons grateful for a refill.

"She's new. Seems nice enough, if a bit young." Stated Andrea.

"Janelle is not that young. Would you believe she is almost thirty? A face like that, so unblemished. I think she just looks naïve because she refuses to wear makeup, fresh-faced, and everything. Well, she's a great worker, so I can't complain much. What will you two be having?"

"The special, please!" We both cried out in unison. The Wellington came with a side of haricots verts, a fancy name for buttered green beans, and potatoes au gratin. I was drooling with abandon.

"Coming right up. Oh! I heard you two were investigating again. I might have some info for you...but let me get your order in first. Sweet tea?"

We nodded yes, and I wondered again at how fast the gossip machine was in this town. I also speculated just what information Sheila could have for us. I guess we were about to find out. Janelle whisked by our table, setting a basket with sweet rolls down with a tiny white bowl filled with butter packets. I took the time to examine her face close up, but I still couldn't see any indication that she was a grown woman about to turn thirty. She looked younger, but she had five years on me!

Good genetics, I surmised.

We didn't have to wait much longer before Sheila came out with our tray laden with delectable goodies. Setting everything in front of us, she glanced around the restaurant, checking that no one needed anything before taking the seat next to Andrea.

"I will be quick because I probably will be called to pick up an order. So here goes. You need to corner that crazy girl and ask her to spill the beans on what she knows. I guarantee the answer lies with her."

Crazy girl? Oh! "You mean Rowan?"

Nodding yes, Sheila leaned close and dropped her voice to a whisper. "She's not right in the head. She was caught up in all that Edith stuff. Well...you need to corner her and find out what else she knows."

"But Sheila. The Council had pronounced her freed from whatever possession took over her. We can't suspect the poor thing just because she was victimized by whatever the puppet-master pulling her strings has done! That wouldn't be fair."

"You can certainly go question her because of what I witnessed last week."

I sat back and watched a self-satisfied look wash over Sheila's face. "I saw Rowan talking to Harley Jacobs, and he didn't look none too happy about what she was a-sayin' to him. As a matter of fact, I thought for a minute he was going to haul off and slap the girl. Three days later, he winds up dead. Now, do you think she warrants a talking to?"

"Hurry up and finish your lunch, Andrea. We have an appointment to get a nightingale to sing!"

Andrea gave me a wicked grin while Sheila gave us a double thumbs-up before heading over to greet some new diners.

Well, well. Isn't this an interesting turn of events? Maybe Rowan was the mysterious figure in Harley's truck!

CHAPTER 12

W hen we entered Fox Den Herbals, we came face to face with a highly flustered Rowan Nightingale, and a rather perturbed Samantha Fairburn, her aunt. To make matters worse, we hadn't even had a chance to open our mouths when Adriana walked in. She informed us she was well ahead in her investigation and had heard about Rowan from several sources. She wasn't forthcoming on just how she received her information, but I suspected she had her minions in the town's rumor mill.

"I don't think any of you have the right to come in here with your insinuations and disturb Rowan so. How is hearsay enough to warrant such a visit, anyway?"

Samantha was not about to give an inch, despite our having my great-grandmother in tow—her reputation proceeds her.

"Samantha. We'd just like to question Rowan about something that has come to light. I mean, would you rather it be the police? I can pass the info on..."

"I know you are no longer with Brian Chase, so don't

pretend you are sharing information back and forth on this matter."

She had a point.

"I meant, we can easily inform Sheriff Buford that Rowan was seen with the victim a few days before he was murdered, and it looked like they had had words between them. That's fine with us. I'm sure Glen would be happy to have a new lead."

Two could play at this game.

Rowan stood behind the counter, twisting the hem of her sweater over and over and biting her lower lip so hard I was amazed it hadn't started bleeding!

"Stop! Wait. No police. Ask your questions. Please, Aunt Sam. I don't want to talk to anyone at the police station!"

Samantha frowned and stood by her niece, placing her hands on her shoulders to center her and calm her nerves. Rowan was a basket case. Understandable considering all that had happened to her recently. But if she did have something to do with this, we couldn't let the fact that she was a victim in the past let her get away with anything this time around.

"Rowan, honey...we aren't trying to make you upset. But you have to understand our position. We've heard from quite a few people that you had words with Harley Jacobs, and it looked heated. Then he winds up dead a few days later. Obviously, we need to clear this up." Andrea was playing good cop, it seems.

Surprisingly, Adriana didn't seem to have anything to add but kept wandering around the shop picking things up and replacing them, mumbling to herself. It was a distraction, and if that was her intent, it was working. Both Samantha and her niece kept following my granny with their eyes, and they couldn't seem to stay focused on us.

"Did you have words with him? With Harley? You have to

understand that a nineteen-year-old young lady arguing with a forty-five-year-old man, someone she doesn't particularly know, seems rather suspicious. So that's why we are asking you these questions." I quantified, trying to gauge how she was reacting to my line of questioning.

"But that's just it. I *do* know...did...did know Harley. His mom and dad have the farm, and I would visit the cows when I wanted to get away from people. They never minded, and I'd just talk to them and pet them. I'd see Harley from time to time, and he was always nice to me."

"What was the argument about the other day? Was he upset at you for some reason?" Andrea gently probed.

Rowan looked down at the floor and quietly whispered her reply, "Harley found some items that he'd stored in the barn attic. Some old mementos and photos and stuff. I was in the barn petting the cows as usual. It seems some of the items were missing, and since I was the only one in or around the box that day, he wanted to know if I took them. So, when he saw me walking to work, he stopped and asked me. I got upset and told him I just knew he found the items because he'd told me about them when he was bringing them down from the attic. But I never saw what was in there! I never looked. I wouldn't open someone's private box!" Rowan paused to look at Adriana, who was now sniffing some of the dried herbs hanging from the rafters in one corner of the shop.

Samantha rolled her eyes and went to see if she could entice my great-grandmother into a purchase since it seemed Rowan was comfortable speaking to Andrea and me.

"You have to understand. Harley was the one who was excited when he found whatever he found. I don't think he even realized he was telling me about what was in the box...it was more like excited chattering, and I was an afterthought to share this discovery with. Then Harley set the box down and went to finish with the milking. After I left, he must have discovered something was missing, or maybe he only thought whatever he had was in there in the first place. I told him I would never do such a thing. We argued a bit about it, but then he agreed that it did seem unlikely I'd take it. But, well, I don't even know what it is! He never said. And now he's gone."

I believed her. I know you shouldn't make assumptions or go on gut instinct because what if Rowan was a masterful actress? However, I didn't think she was lying to us in this instance. However, I wondered if she was telling us the whole truth. It did leave more questions than it answered. If Rowan hadn't taken items out of the box I now had in my possession, did that mean someone else did? Someone who may have been watching Rowan petting the cows that day and just happened to see Harley when he discovered his old mementos. But that would be way too coincidental, and I didn't believe in coincidences.

Perhaps Harley mentioned his find to someone after the fact. And later on, that night, they snuck into the barn and took the items? Or the next day? Without Harley here to question, we'd never know. I was about to thank Rowan and leave when Adriana sidled up to the counter and gave the girl a stern look. Samantha was straightening the herbs in the corner and hadn't noticed yet.

"Young lady, did you or did you not put a spell on the Jacobs's cows so their milk would start to dry up? Just a friendly question, mind you. I'm curious about these things."

What? Where did that come from?

Rowan had gone pale and looked as if she were about to pass out.

"I... no. I wouldn't...you have it wrong," uttered Rowan softly.

"Then perhaps you'd care to explain? I'm so old, you see,

and get confused easily. But I did hear Mrs. Jacobs complaining to Doc Holcomb about the strange phenomenon with their cows seeming not to produce like they used to, and he checked them out but found nothing wrong with them." Adriana began toying with a few items on the counter while Rowan tracked her movements with her eyes, sweat beading on her forehead. "That is until they happened to look down finding sage on the floor of the barn." Adriana continued.

"I also noted you were walking along the road heading toward their farm, and you always had a basket with you. Sometimes you could use sage to dry up a cow's milk, and I notice you seem to be out of it here. You usually carry so much of that herb, I just wondered."

"What are you implying? Don't you think I'd notice if we had a huge shortage in stock? I think you had better leave...now!"

Samantha had come back to the counter just in time to hear Adriana's statement, and I guessed she didn't like what she was hearing. With our line of questioning being cut short by her protective aunt, we had no choice but to leave Rowan be and head back out of the shop. But not before Adriana gave one more parting comment. "Truth comes out in the end, dear...remember that. It always does."

"Out!" Samantha followed us to the door, then shut and locked it behind us, flipping the sign from open to closed. I wondered if we had just made an enemy, but I couldn't worry about that if it meant getting to the bottom of Harley's murder.

"Well, that was fun, kids." In the light of day, Adriana's outfit left a lot to be desired. She had added to her investigator's garb, and now she had a long cardigan sweater, but it was two sizes too big, so she did look like a tiny bat.

"Fun? I don't think that was *fun* at all," griped Andrea, "I think we may have lost a place to buy our herbs and maybe even other necessities if Rita chooses to stick by her employee."

"Bah. I was just messing with that kid. I ran into Harley's mother about a week before he passed, and she told me Rowan had been pulling wild sage for the shop and managed to drop her basket in the barn...the poor kid was scrambling, trying to get everything picked up and away from the cows. I know she didn't do anything to hurt either them or Harley...but she knows something about that box. Mark my words. Something or someone is keeping her from talking. This was just a ploy to rattle her a bit. Let's see where it leads."

"I hope it leads somewhere. I'm stumped at this point. Where to next?" I wondered.

Adriana didn't pause but walked over to my...Jeep?

"How did this get here? We walked!"

We trailed along behind her, and I knew she had a plan she wasn't voicing, and now it appears she's taken up grand theft auto as a hobby. Imagine our surprise when we opened the Jeep's doors and found Wicked sitting in the driver seat.

"How the heck did you get in here?"

"Please don't tell me she can drive." Andrea followed and deftly moved around Adriana to claim the front passenger seat. Granny gave her a mulish look but climbed in the back.

"I drove over here. You left your keys in the ignition, smart ass. Here. Take them. I found the cat sitting in front, meowing pitifully. I was going to let her out into your yard and head over, but she refused to leave the Jeep, ducking under the seats out of reach. You need to take better care of her, Liliana. I think she's hungry and seems to be a bit gimpy."

Wicked looked mildly insulted that I scooted her over, but she settled down on Andrea's lap, curled up in a tiny ball after a few moments of kneading, and seemed to be preparing to take a nap.

OK, then. Wicked didn't look weak or crippled to me.

"Head over to Woodpecker Lane." Commanded Adriana imperiously from the back seat.

"What's on Woodpecker Lane?"

"Not what. *Who.* We are going to pay Olivia a little visit. She has been avoiding me, and I suspect she may surmise I found out about her meddling with our little family drama. I want to ask her if she was looking into who removed those spells on our behalf, or did she have a more sinister motive."

"She has no thumbs," Andrea stated.

"Who? Olivia?"

"No. Not Olivia. Wicked. She has no thumbs. How did she manage to get in your Jeep?"

"Even if she *had* thumbs. Look at the size of her tiny paws. No way could she manage to open these doors. How does she keep doing these things?"

"She's a magical cat," sniffed Adriana, "what's the big deal?"

"The big deal is she's just a cat who happens to be housing my mother. Neither of them can open a door in their current state. So, how does she keep doing stuff?"

I saw my great-grandmother roll her eyes through my visor mirror and frowned.

I was about to pull out into traffic, but suddenly I thought of something that had me slamming on my brakes, rocking my passengers forward along with Wicked, who would have most assuredly fallen to the floor had Andrea not grabbed and steadied her.

"Hey! You're going to knock my dentures out!"

"The dagger!"

"What? Lily, what is wrong?" Andrea asked.

"The dagger. Who has the dagger? And you don't wear dentures, so stop playing the victim, old lady."

"Why, that would be...hey! Tanaquil told me she had passed it on to Olivia. How fortuitous! We can kill two birds with one stone," Adriana smiled darkly.

"We will head to Olivia's house, then. But first, I need to return this cat home. Not that I remotely think she will stay there if she doesn't want to."

We made the short trip to my place, and everyone followed me to the back door, Andrea snuggling Wicked in her arms. That's where I stopped short in surprise and had everyone bumping into me in short order.

"Ouch! Why did you stop moving?" Andrea was prying Wicked's claws from her shoulder and peered around me to see what the holdup was.

I couldn't move. I was astounded, and I couldn't believe what I was seeing. The sweetbriar rose bush outside my back door that had been a sickly, yet overgrown shrub was now neatly trimmed into a pleasant-looking bush. All the dead canes had removed, giving the outwards facing buds room to bloom and grow. I could see the white pith in the healthy stems and even noticed someone had mulched the base. The pruning shears remained on the bottom step, and all the old debris was sitting in a neat pile, waiting for disposal.

"Look at the bush."

"Yeah. We're looking. What gives? You did a nice job pruning it, by the way."

"That's just it, Granny. I didn't prune it. I thought for a minute that you did. Why else were you here?"

"I didn't touch it. I came over to see if you were here, but before I could get to the back door, I heard that cat making a racket in the vehicle. As I went over to check it out, Sheila texted me where you were heading, so I took your Jeep and left. I didn't even glance at the bush."

"Someone even watered it." Andrea pointed out.

Adriana went over to the shrub and bent down, examining the work.

"That isn't water."

Andrea wrinkled her forehead and bent over next to my great-grandmother.

"What's with all the flies? Isn't it early in the season for them to be out and about? Although it has been warming up a bit. So, if it isn't water, what is it?" Andrea began itching her elbow again.

Adriana glanced at me and said, "Hold her."

"What do you mean? Hold who?"

"Oh my gosh! That's, that's blood!" Screeched Andrea, who had reached out and touched the ground at the base of the trimmed shrub. She pulled her hand away, and it was covered in a sticky brownish pink residue that could only be one thing.

"Blood? That explains the flies. But whose blood...gah!"

Thud.

Down went Andrea yet again.

Oh. Hold *Andrea.* Well, it was a bit late for that now.

* * *

"I'M FINE... I'm fine. Sorry, it was just so unexpected."

Andrea, hands freshly washed, sat in my den rocking back and forth slightly and still looked a bit green for my liking.

We had managed to carry Andrea into my house and deposited her on the sofa. Wicked trotted upstairs like she didn't have a care in the world. Leaving Andrea propped in an ungainly position, Adriana and I had reconvened outside with a trowel and plastic baggy, gathering some of the dirt up to have tested. We needed to know whose blood that was, or at least have it as evidence of...what, really? It's not like this was a crime scene.

"Someone was here, Granny. Someone trimmed this bush and left these tools out. I don't even own tools. Why, though? What is so important about this bush? And is this why Wicked was out and about? Did someone let her out?" My voice was getting higher with every question, and I knew I probably sounded agitated.

Wicked had protected the shrub from utter devastation a few weeks back when I renovated my house. One of the workers who turned out to be a murderous tool that did away with his nephew for weird, twisted reasons had tried to cut it down. Only Wicked had prevented each attempt in a feline display of pure fiendish terror. Her antics had all the remaining workers giving her a wide berth.

Heading back inside, we found Andrea sitting up, rubbing her head, having just come back from freshening up in my half bath. She stopped massaging her head and placed her hand on her stomach like she was feeling ill.

"You aren't going to be sick, are you? My floors..."

My heart of pine flooring had been fully restored but kept taking one minor incident after another as of late, and I fretted at the likelihood of them remaining unsullied. Wicked had tossed those peas and dirt everywhere, I flung pizza which landed on it, and I had ghost issues that had caused other incidents, not to mention a massive tree branch making an appearance in my upper hall—yet another long story. I have so many. I had a feeling any day now, I would be dealing with damaged and besmirched wood.

"Can't get blood off a floor that ain't sealed."

"Holy, Abner!"

Old Frank's brother, and my sometime handyman, Abner, had just appeared in my kitchen, not only scaring me once again but reading my thoughts in the process. Abner was a walking nuisance that always seemed to be one step ahead of me with grating one-liners that made him an annoying Captain Obvious at times. He wasn't as grizzled as his brother, but he reminded me of every old codger you'd see in old black and white movies that would show up, make a dire pronouncement, then leave.

I wish he'd leave now.

I spun around to confront the cagey man only to find him standing behind me in the entrance to the mudroom, and he was holding a long, sharp dagger in his hand that was dripping with fresh blood.

Thud.

Well, it looks like we lost Andrea... *again.*

CHAPTER 13

*a*fter awakening to a face full of cold water, thanks to Adriana, Andrea had shakily gathered around the table with me in the sunporch. I knew my pine floors would suffer.

Abner was sitting with us, the dagger laying on newspaper that he spread out. He was explaining his appearance and the dagger in hand.

"Found it on the ground near that rose bush."

"But how did you happen to be here? Why did you come over?"

"Heard you needed a tiller. You got to get them peas in."

Oh. Well, that was sweet. I guess.

"You bought me a tiller?"

"Nope."

"You're lending me your tiller?"

"Nope."

"OK, Abner...where did the tiller come from then?"

"That mechanic of yours dropped it off and had me get it up and running for you."

Lorcan! That explained his trip to the hardware store in

Clayton. I should have realized he wouldn't shop there unless Dennis didn't carry an item his shop. Mystery solved. If only they were all so easy.

"Thank you for doing that, Abner. As for the dagger, it looks like the same one I discovered, and we turned over to the Council."

Abner gave me a long look.

"Could be."

"But if that's true, how did it come to be back here? Wasn't it being tested for tracing remnants? That means Olivia definitely has some explaining to do. Like heaps!"

Abner just shrugged.

"But this makes no sense!"

"Sometimes, the things that make the least bit o' sense are the things that make the most sense once enough time has passed," Abner stated like a wizened sage.

That was almost prophetic. I think.

"This is the same dagger." Adriana proclaimed, looking at my ceiling with seemed interest. "Where did that cat go?"

"Why do you want my cat? Don't you even think of hurting her!" I cried. Wicked could be the bane of my existence, but I didn't want her to come into any harm. After all, she made a great foot-warmer, and just last week, she cornered a tiny mouse in the mudroom. She even held it and waited for me to open the back door so we could let it out. Hey, we were pacifists at heart. Although I did spend the entire time screaming and searching for a broom, so I'm not sure if the mouse would have made it had I found one before we freed the critter.

Just then, Wicked came sauntering back into the kitchen and spying us in the sunporch, adjusted her path, and wandered in. She hopped onto her window seat and sat, blinking calmly at us. That was until Adriana scooped her up and began examining her. Because then it turned into some kind of holy hell that you only witness if you happened to an extra in a horror movie.

Andrea ran screaming from the room while I tried to remove Wicked from the back of Abner's head—she jumped on him to escape my great-grandmother. Adriana was hurling curses, the word kind, not the spell kind, at my cat, who was snarling while Abner tried to pull her off. The shrieking was intense—Abner's, not Wicked's.

Jake and Lorcan came busting through the back door, the latter wielding a baseball bat and the former holding a two-by-four leftover from construction.

If that wasn't bad enough, Edith chose that moment to pop in.

She took one wide-eyed look at the hullabaloo and popped right back out again.

Chicken.

I finally managed to wrangle my cat off Abner and calm her down enough that she deigned to allow Adriana to give her a once over. My great-grandmother nodded and then shot me a weighted stare as if deciding how much news I could handle. It was making me nervous.

The men settled down, and Abner had backed out of the room then scurried off after leaving a pamphlet on how to operate the tiller. I felt terrible about the cat attack and hoped he would get those claw marks examined. And a stitch or two.

"What the holy heck is wrong with that cat?" Jake asked, giving Wicked a wary look and keeping his distance. She was currently giving herself a full-body wash to straighten her rumpled fur.

"She's had twenty years of being inhabited by a dark witch. Quite frankly, I think she's doing rather well—all things considered." I was choosing optimism.

"She's mentally unstable."

Thank you, Adriana.

"Maybe if you stopped grabbing her and doing invasive examinations on her person..."

"Person? She's a cat and not much of one. You have mice."

"I am perfectly aware of that. We've decided to get little Have-a-Heart traps and..."

"What kind of dark witch goes around saving mini rats? Blast them with magic and call it a day!"

"I would rather not have to...why are you even worried about...how can I get anything done when..."

"Didn't they teach you how to complete a sentence at that fancy college you went to up North?"

"Oh, don't start with me, you old hag. I will have you know..."

"Whoa! Please stop it. Both of you. You do realize you fight so much because you are exactly alike, right? It's unnerving," shouted Jake, quieting the two of us instantly.

"I'm nothing like her. She whines and pouts and acts like a teenager." Adriana followed this up by blowing a rather loud raspberry.

"Oh, that's the pot calling the kettle blue."

"Black."

"What?"

"Calling the kettle black. You said it incorrectly."

"Black, blue...someone will most assuredly be black and blue if they don't shut it."

"Enough!" Lorcan came between the two of us and walked me into the kitchen.

"I do *not* act like a teenager! I've been through so much since I've lost my mom, Aunt Jessica. Argh!" I stomped into the dining room, through the living room, and ran up the flight of stairs to the second level running into my bedroom, slamming the door.

OK, maybe that was a tad teen-like, but I was over this. Let them figure it out. I was going to sulk in my bed and...

That's when I noticed the blood drips across the floor leading from my private bath.

* * *

"IF YOU LOOK, you can see that most of the blood is in the sink, then drips on the floor leading out to the landing and down the steps to the foyer. That's where it stops until you notice a tiny drip in the dining room and another in the kitchen and the bloody thumbprint still on my back doorknob."

Everyone was following me around the house as I played this macabre show-and-tell of a blood trail through my home. Even Adriana had looked impressed when I followed with my discovery and revelation.

"I thought to quickly cast my tracking spell on the fresh blood in the sink...and I nailed it using the strongest Shadow Dancer magic I know. I'm so glad Tanaquil took the time to show me a bit more regarding my talent."

"What did you find, Lily?" Andrea asked breathlessly.

"I know whose blood it is without a doubt."

I went over to my favorite chair in the den and sat. Everyone following and taking the other seats with Jake perching on the hearth near my fireplace.

"It belongs to my mom. To Adelaide."

"Well, we could have guessed that. I already told you I spied a tiny cut on that cat of yours, Her pad, on her paw. Somehow Wicked must have..."

"No. Granny...no. The thumbprint isn't one of ours. It belongs to Adelaide. It's *her* print. Which means somehow, sometime today, she was freed from being a prisoner inside Wicked and walked through my home."

My pronouncement was met with total silence until Wicked chose that moment to sneeze.

All eyes turned to my cat, who returned our look with one of derisive ennui. Then Wicked turned tail and trotted over to the back door, jumped up to open the knob, and continued to the side yard. We all followed as she wandered over to the bush and sat.

"Mreow?"

"What is it about this bush? Forget the amazing for the moment that Adelaide was here, and most likely cut her hand and let her blood soak into the earth around this bush. The question is *why*? How, and why?" I pondered.

"Lily? Remember the story June told us? The one about Jess, Addy, Charlie, and her? When they were kids playing by Nichols Pond?" Andrea slowly began to speak, then as she warmed up to her story, she became excited.

"Oh my gosh! Charlie! His nickname was *Rosy* because he enjoyed tending Antonio's rose bushes and would bring the girls' roses. What if this bush is tied to him somehow?"

I blinked, and then a slow smile crept over my face. "Andrea, you may have something here. But in what way is he tied to it?"

I hadn't noticed Adriana kneeling before the sweetbriar rose until she began carefully digging through the dirt with her hands. Wicked watched her warily but didn't try and stop what she was doing.

"What is it? What do you think you will find?"

Adriana didn't answer but began to frantically dig faster and faster until I thought she meant to uproot the newly pruned shrub. Suddenly she cried out and sat back on her haunches.

Jake leaned down, frowning, then placed a hand on my great-grandmother's shoulder, offering a hand to help her stand once more.

"What is that? A doll of some sort?" Asked Lorcan as he rubbed his neck and stared down at the little item poking up out of the ground.

"It's a poppet," Adriana stated dully.

"Like a voodoo doll or something?" I asked, frustrated at my continued naivety.

"A bit. Not unlike a voodoo doll, but more sympathetic magic, not destructive magic," Adriana explained, wiping the dirt off on her pants, "a voodoo doll is more sinister. This tiny poppet represents Charlie, and if my suspicions are correct, Adelaide, or the cat anyway, is performing some kind of ritual magic to keep Charlie alive—with her blood sacrifice."

This discovery could not be a good thing. *Right?*

CHAPTER 14

*A*driana called in the troops. This time we had not only family and friends present, but the police. Sheriff Glen Buford accompanied by a wary Brian Chase, listened in amazement to our tale. That his Great Aunt Olivia had played some role in the attempted removal of the reversal spell that Edith told us about had him concerned. Planning a way to approach and question her that he could handle delicately—and without the knowledge of the other Elders was making him ill. He was trying to protect her, yet I could tell he'd see justice served if she had played any part in the destruction of my family.

I hoped she had a good reason and didn't turn out to be an enemy. I rather liked the imposing older woman who had pronounced me a highly talented dark witch after my trials.

Adriana had carefully removed the poppet from the ground with gloved hands under the watchful eye of Wicked. She became uninterested in the proceedings once the item was in my house and away from the rose bush. It was gently wrapped in a linen cloth and sitting on my coffee table.

Brian examined the poppet and was the only one who

had noticed writing across the back of it, although none of us knew what it could mean:

> Words are no matter;
> only glass will blood shatter
> Draught of elderberry,
> mixed with strands of heir
> Take this poppet to open the lair
> Curse reversed, and all is well
> The one who is left standing…
> …is sacrificed to Hell

"Shouldn't that be hair? Like, it's a riddle, but it isn't spelled correctly," I wondered.

Adriana kept reading the lines over and over again. Someone sewed them onto the fabric of the little figure in what appeared to be golden thread. She frowned when Brian leaned over and snapped a photo of the inscription with his phone, but didn't stop him from doing so.

As my relatives and friends arrived, I decided to offer an impromptu dinner, so I glanced at Lorcan. He picked up on my thoughts right away. "Pizza? Maybe I should order us a bunch?"

"Yes, darling. That would be perfect. Henry, be a dear and go run over to our place and bring a case of soda and a case of beer," Eileen Reid, Lorcan's mom, suggested, and Jake quickly offered to go with Henry and lend a hand. Lorcan went into the kitchen to place our pizza order. "Get some salads too, sweetie!" Eileen instructed Lorcan, then turned to me, patting my hand.

Cousin Flora had shown up with her mother, Sophia, and she rushed to help Andrea as she began clearing the dining room table and set paper plates and napkins all around. Aunt Iona was in shock and being comforted by my

Uncle Owen. Aunt Chiara, Andrea's mother, sat on her other side.

"Should I call me mum, do you think?" Iona's Scot accent made a slight appearance in her distressed state as she began to fuss with the hem of her blouse.

"Not yet, dear. We need to know more about what is going on. Once we have those answers, we can decide what to say," stated Aunt Chiara.

My Aunt Iona turned to me, then looked back at Aunt Chiara, then smiled. "If it weren't for our Lily here, we wouldn't have grown so close like we used to be, Chiara. I am so happy she brought both sides of the family together again, just like old times. But, well, almost. If we can just get Adelaide and Charlie back."

And she was off sobbing again.

I felt my anger building. Who was doing this to my family...and why? It couldn't just be Donna Fredricks at this point. Even from her command base deep inside the vaults of the Council prison, she had to have help, and there had to be a connection between the renegade Romano witches. I stood and entered the kitchen, finding Lorcan and my Uncle Owen conversing in low voices with Brian and Sheriff Glen.

"Brian, I don't know what is going on with your aunt, and I am not sure if I should be so trusting of you, but despite our differences..."

"Lily, we don't have any differences..." I held up my hand to forestall any more comments.

"Despite that, I can't believe you would do anything to hurt me. But I'm not so sure regarding your great aunt. What is her story? Would she be holding any grudges against my family?"

"She is my father's mother's aunt—sister to my great-grandmother. My dad never spoke much about his parents. They died young and in similar circumstances to your grandparents...an automobile accident. My grandmother, Mallory, was an Ogden. Apparently, the Ogden's never wanted to marry into the Chase family, but nothing could keep Mallory and my grandfather Phillip apart. Their only child was my dad, Dillon. We are not very lucky people, it seems. You know what happened with my father."

Dillon had hung himself after Adelaide disappeared, and Jessica ran away with me. Everyone believed he was despondent over the loss of Adelaide, even though he was married to Rita by that time with young son Brian around six or seven. Brian found his father hanging from a tree down by the banks of the Coleman River. My heart just bled for that little boy every time I remembered the story. Especially since Adelaide, my mother, had such a role to play in it, albeit minimal. They had had one rendezvous when Rita was pregnant with Brian, and Adelaide was barely seventeen. A transgression she regretted, and one Dillon should have known better than to pursue.

My mother was a free spirit and bewitching—despite being a witch. Her hair was supposedly multi-shades of fiery reds with golden highlights, and she had intense eyes flecked with bronze. The more I looked at her photos, the more I could see what everyone had been saying, that I favored her, although I was raven-haired with cognac brown eyes like my dad Charlie. I did have my mother's skin; I was pale, deathly so at times. However, I'd tan in the summer and not suffer the usual pale-skinned tendency to burn, thanks to my Italian side. I wondered if we shared similar mannerisms.

"Do you think Olivia holds a grudge against Adelaide because of what your dad and she, um..." I trailed off lamely, not sure of how to ask such a delicate question. This couldn't be easy for Brian, either.

"Olivia holds grudges like a Jewish mother whose son moved to another state to be near his new wife's family."

Adriana had come up behind us, adding her two cents.

I knew Granny held a bit of animosity as far as Olivia was concerned. The two had been in diapers together, and Olivia always liked to point out that she was the older and wiser of the duo. But theirs seemed to be a friendly sort of rivalry, and I didn't hold much credence to any truly hostile rancor between them.

"Or an old Italian witch whose nose gets out of joint over any perceived slight and makes everyone's life miserable wherever she goes?" I returned, giving her a look.

"You have a point."

"I do?" I asked incredulously.

"I'm Italian. We hold grudges...a vendetta. It's part and parcel of who we are."

Well. OK, then.

"I've invited her over," Adriana stated, wrapping the poppet up once more and tucking it into the drawer in my end table.

"Who? Olivia? You reached her on the phone, finally?"

"I have. She will be here momentarily. Keep that poppet safe. Please don't mess with it. Just leave it wrapped in there for now."

I saw Brian's eyes widen at the news his great aunt was on the way, and he seemed to deflate a little. I knew Olivia could be complex and tended to run roughshod over her relatives. I know Rita managed to avoid her whenever she could. I wondered if she had returned from wherever it was she'd been. I'd have to ask Brian before he left.

There was a mystery around his mother that concerned Dennis Carter, Jake's dad, that had a few of us wondering if they had been having an affair. I say had because after an incident Lorcan and I witnessed over the holidays, we think they may have called it off. Good for my dear friend, June,

Jake's mom, who didn't need to be treated in such a way, if indeed it was an affair.

The Carter's were here tonight as well, and June came over to me, pulling me away from everyone.

"I need a word with you, Lily."

June looked fraught with emotion that gave me pause. What on earth could have her so rattled? I followed her into my sunporch, where she spun around, closing the glass doors to give us some privacy.

"Lily, I just heard from the...um...a friend that something strange has happened, and I don't know if I should say anything just yet."

By friend, I assumed it was someone on the highly active gossip mill.

"What is it, June? What's wrong?"

"Well...you see, that's just it. I am not sure if anything is wrong or I am overreacting or believing nonsensical rumors. I thought to ask you if I should make an announcement or if I should verify the truth before spreading a rumor too fantastic to believe."

Now she had my attention. "What rumor? What did you hear?"

I didn't comment when I noticed the ghost of Edith Plank emerge from behind June and swirl around to face her. Edith was becoming such a fixture that it barely registered when she turned to me and professed she was worried at how ashen June looked. I just nodded my head which June took to be me encouraging her to speak.

"I just got off the phone with Shirley."

Shirley Jones was our resident E.M.T. and ringleader of the Gossip Girls. It figures she'd have something juicy to pass on. "I don't know if she is playing a practical joke, and I am the butt of it, but she said...well, she told me just now that..."

"What do you mean he's missing?! How could a body go

missing...no correct that how could another body go missing?"

June and I looked askance at each other as Brian's voice carried to where we were standing. Edith raised both of her hands to her cheeks and made an 'O' shape with her mouth. Brian had his phone to his ear, and he was pacing back and forth in my kitchen, with Sheriff Glen standing by looking thunderstruck. Whatever it was, it didn't sound good.

June turned back to me after glancing at the troubled detective, owl-eyed and colorless. "Oh my...I guess the rumor is true."

"What is it? Is what Brian is yelling about the same thing you are trying to tell me?"

"Oh, Lily. This can't be happening again, but it looks like it's true. Shirley informed me that a fellow ambulance worker friend told her that Harley Jacobs's body went missing! It was to be released today to his parents so they could bury him tomorrow, but it's gone! They showed up to claim him and sign papers and had Chester Soule ready with his hearse...only when they arrived in Gwinnett County, Harley was nowhere!"

With those words, Edith evaporated in a puff of smoke.

How do you like that? And this time, Bubba and Donna couldn't be the body snatchers. Which bellies the question, who could have taken Harley Jacobs...and why?

CHAPTER 15

We were all sprawled around my home, most of my friends and family in the dining room—pizza boxes open with the tasty offerings and salads enjoyed by all. A few had moved to the formal living room doing the same. This way, we could all hear what was being tossed around in theory. Brian had left with the sheriff, and we had welcomed Olivia, who joined us not with a sense of nervous guilt, but one of resigned acceptance.

"I do believe Harley Jacobs ties to the events of the past, and his murder was an attempt to stop him from revealing something to Lily and you, Adriana," stated Olivia.

She was wearing a severe grey dress, wool, with a shawl around her shoulders. Her hair was silver, and her eyes were a cerulean blue deeper but just as vibrant as Brian's. "I worked for years without the knowledge of the Council, trying to discover who had breached the lower levels of the library. I knew they couldn't get in by normal means since Charles had sealed it. So, I assume they used a transport key like I had fashioned with Edith to allow her to reach the lower levels. Edith lost hers. Someone must have made another in case the Council sealed the forbidden level. So now, it is safe to assume there are two such keys."

We all listened in rapt attention as she told her bleak tale.

"I knew Deanna and Donna did not possess the power to perform such magics as they were purported to have done. Once the evil doings surrounding this family came to light when Lily returned to Sweet Briar, it brought all my old investigations back to the forefront. I asked Edith, who was head of the library still, just weeks before dying, to try once more to find where someone might have hidden the passages removed from the spellbook in question. You see, there is no way Deanna could have removed the page she tore from the book out of the lower levels. The result would have been cataclysmic. It is down there still, hidden somewhere. What she and her sister did manage to get away with was conceal-ment of their lineage that allowed them to pull off quite the deception and destruction of your family, Adriana, and yours, Iona."

Lineage? What was Olivia saying?

"I don't understand why these women have such hatred for my family," said Adriana, "they were presented to me at the Trials and deemed inadequate witches. Weak and of no substance. It is not my fault; however, I could see that they'd regarded me as someone who didn't allow them to have a greater position. But what could I do? They aren't, well, they didn't seem powerful. It disturbs and angers me that they deceived me."

"Who are they anyway? I mean, where do they come from? I know they have ties to the Buford's. Donna gave Bubba, um, Beau, that surname instead of his father's. But it always made me confused because she is a Fredricks, not a Buford...right?" Andrea asked.

"Those Buford and Fredricks are all related in some way. Cousins marrying cousins. Not close, but close enough that they are all tied somehow," stated Dennis Carter, piping up where he'd been mostly quiet, "nothing against the sheriff, but that family is a hodge-podge of intertwined genetics. Which probably explains the psychotic actions of those two women!"

"Bad breeding cannot be the sole reason to blame those two for what they've done. This is a driving force of hatred so deep it boggles the mind. Why, though? I cannot understand why they hate us so!" Aunt Chiara cried out.

"I want to know how someone as nice as Harley could fall for a harlot like Deanna. She was so promiscuous and blatant about it; I don't know how that poor man suffered all these years yet still held her memory in such high regard that he never married. And now, not only is he dead, he's missing! What on earth is going on around here?" stated June with such vehemence it shocked me until I remembered how close she was to Harley's mom.

"The rumors going around town back then had Deanna running off to Atlanta several times to take care of some of her transgressions. I wonder how many times she terminated a pregnancy. Did Harley ever know? She would disappear from time to time, sometimes for months. She may even have had a few babies and gave them up for adoption. That would have been a blessing if she did."

Olivia seemed to be listening to everyone with an air of suppressed knowledge of something that would most definitely shock us once she revealed all. But it seems she was content to let us continue to ponder. For now, anyway.

"And now he's missing. This is insanity. How could his body get up and disappear out of the morgue? Who was in charge...oh. Wait. Yolanda." I grimaced. I hope the medical examiner would be reprimanded severely by higher-ups. How she could have a body disappear from her watch, under her very nose, was beyond me. A petty little part of me hoped she'd be dealt with severely.

Olivia looked at me with interest. "Yolanda, did you say? Who is this person to you? Why mention that name?"

I stared at Brian's great aunt in consternation. Was she not aware that her nephew is dating the medical examiner in charge of Harley Jacobs's body? Perhaps not. I don't go around discussing my love life with every relative. Why should Brian?

"Yolanda Serrano. She is the new medical examiner in Gwinnett County and is in charge of Harley's body. She is the one who called it murder and pronounced him dead at the scene."

While I explained, I observed the ghost of Moira Muir Fortune appear behind Adriana. She seemed to be sitting in midair, and when she caught my glance, gave me another little wink. What I found even more fascinating was the look on Olivia's face. She, too, it seemed, could see my newest spectral visitor, nodded at her in greeting even, yet she remained quiet. Interesting.

Olivia turned to me again, not addressing the ghost in the room. "Serrano? Serrano. Now, why does that name sound familiar?"

I was about to expound on the relationship between Brian and the hated medical examiner when Olivia's eyes lit up, and she turned to Adriana once more. "How curious and alarming. I need to tell you all a story, and when completed, I think you will understand more of this entire sordid tale."

Adriana nodded at her to continue.

"Now, you have to understand. What I am about to tell you I've only confirmed very recently and with the utmost discretion. I'd not told you yet because I have become distracted with this ridiculous upheaval at the prison; how Donna

Fredricks managed to escape to the lowest levels and create a small army is beyond me. The Council, as some of you well know, have been trying to decide if we need to move the other prisoners out and create a new facility. Then they want to hit the lower levels with enough magic to eradicate everything. But, as usual, we are dealing with red-tape and politics," grumbled Olivia. She fussed with the napkin in front of her.

I was shocked, studying my relatives who were Elders and noting the frustration they must all be experiencing at the hands of the other Council members.

Olivia continued, "when I had Edith search me in the forbidden library, and then heard she died, I immediately delved deeper into my research. I knew that young witch, Rowan Nightingale, had been possessed. It got me to thinking about any past stories of such a thing happening to one of our own, and I went looking for answers."

Olivia sat back and gave each of us a calculated look, then continued,

"I found them."

At this point, we were all transfixed upon the elderly witch whose demeanor went from a confident narrator to a woman who seemed fragile. I looked with concern at my great-grandmother, who reached out to her contemporary with apprehension.

"Olivia. What is this? What did you learn?"

"What I am about to tell you will hurt this family. Please let me get the entire story out in one sitting; no interruptions." When she saw we all nodded our acceptance to her request, she told her story.

"Magaigh and Moira Muir, your grandmother and great aunt, respectively, Lily, grew up in Scotland, and each married Scottish lads. Magaigh, Maggie, married Reginald Croy. Moira married Robert Fortune. Before Maggie married Reginald, a week before the big day, as a matter of fact, young Moira was walking home from the village church when another Croy attacked her; Rorie. He was Reginald's younger brother, a brutish thug who had a reputation for petty crimes and boorish behavior. The Croy family had disowned the lad, and he was living the life of a ruffian on the streets.

"Moira never told anyone what had happened, except for her future brother-in-law, Reginald. He gave his brother the beating of his life and sent him away, telling him to never return to the family or disgrace their name ever again. When Rorie departed, he left his wife behind...oh yes, he had married a village girl and set up house not too far from his family farm, despite the rift. The poor girl admitted to a year of physical and mental abuse at the hands of her husband once he was out of the picture, and she went back home to her family. She swore up and down that Rorie could possess people at will. Her family chalked it off to hysterics, but someone made a note of it in the Council. When I did my research on such things, imagine my surprise to see the Croy name!

To get back to my story, Rorie, it seems, came to the States and took up with a woman who had the reputation of being loose and wanton. He stayed with her for a time, but Rorie decided to go back home to Scotland five years into his dalliance. He never made it. They found Rorie's body in North Carolina in the woods burned and in such a state, it took months to identify him."

Aunt Iona blanched at this news but was nodding her head. "I know this story of my uncle...but only that he was brutally murdered here, and they never caught who did it. I also knew he was the black sheep in the family, and no one here had anything to do with him."

Olivia smiled gently at her then went on with the tale, "The woman he had been having an affair with if you can call it that, was named Dierdre. Dierdre was the bastard child of one of the many Fredricks from North Carolina and a very distant cousin to the Buford clan here in Georgia. Dierdre took the Fredricks surname later in life. Her father never admitted her claim that she was his daughter, but it was a true claim. She bore two children by Rorie Croy, Donna, and Deanna. They are your cousins."

The cry that went out in the room was one of disbelief and anger mixed with shock. I sat back in my chair and found myself tracking my eyes to Moira, who floated to the corner and was watching the faces of her loved ones. She met my eyes and nodded yes.

Olivia held up her hands and shouted over the din, "Please, let me finish." Once everyone settled down, she took up the story once more, "Dierdre forbade the girls ever to mention Rorie's name or that they were, in fact, Croys. More than anything else in this world, Dierdre hated being a witch, and she suppressed both her daughter's abilities with her own magic, causing them to become very weak.

Trust me, with Croy blood in them, as you well know, they would have been substantial had Diedre not done this. She kept them enslaved and living in fear of her wrath. Both of those girls grew up to hate the Croy name and coveted anything their cousins possessed. Especially one cousin who seemed to be the belle of the bunch, the most vivacious and alive of all the cousins they came across Adelaide. More than anything, Donna and Deanna wanted what Adelaide loved with all her heart. Charles Sweet.

"This became a festering obsession. Which culminated in the destruction to your family at the hands of those two depraved women."

I couldn't believe this. I was related to those awful, nasty, dreadful witches. My poor Aunt Jessica even befriended Donna for a time, and she was the evil witch that had convinced Jessica to run away with me to escape some made-up danger. The only ones after me or my family were the two insane sisters. It all made sense now but was just too horrific to contemplate.

"Hang on a second," I protested and turned to Olivia for an explanation, "how did Donna and Deanna get so powerful? If they had their magic suppressed and became weak, how did they get to be so strong? And powerful enough to fool the Council and perform such dark magic on my family?"

"You have just answered your question. How does any power come to witch folk? Family. Jewelry that each family passes down. You are wearing the very jewelry the sisters stole to bring their abilities back. The sweet briar roses were very strongly imbued by the Croy family and belonged to Adelaide. She found them when she was young and always wore them. Your father, Charlie, made her the little sweet briar rose charm that dangles even now on the bracelet you are wearing.

"Of all the pieces Adelaide possessed, however, nothing was stronger than a circlet that her grandfather, Reginald and Rorie's father, had crafted with his own hands and completed the set. It was a gorgeous piece in a Celtic key pattern, with the sweetbriar roses across the center. Donna stole that circlet, and the power transferred to her. Blood. The magic knows the blood."

"Edith heard rumors about it from your cousin Nora. She had been looking into your family for years, trying to piece this all together, and I believe she knows much more than she ever let on. Obviously, Nora wanted the ring you are wearing and tried to get it from the bottom of Nichols Pond. She failed. You succeeded. I think Nora coveted all the pieces, so she'd become the stronger witch, not Lily. Edith helped her because Nora must have promised something in return if she'd help."

Olivia addressed the room at large once again, "Beware, however, for those two women have breached the forbidden library and have learned some very dark magic indeed. The spells used to turn Adelaide and erase Charlie's memories are vile. Ultimately powerful and corrupt. They are still in the library. They must be. And we need to get those pages back if we are ever to begin reversing the spells and reinstate Adelaide, and hopefully get Charlie to awaken from his hellish prison and come back to reality."

Adriana looked sick with worry and angered at the destruction to not only the Dolce clan but to our Croy family as well.

"How did they find out about my Romano relations?"

"That we do not know. But it seems Donna must have found out about them and either sent Charlie to them or released him on his quest, and they laid in wait, capturing him and bringing him to the northwestern part of the country. We do not have those answers yet," finished Olivia.

"What about what we discovered today, the dagger. The fresh blood. Is Adelaide able to free herself from being bound with Wicked?" I asked.

Olivia looked at me, considering my words. "I believe you have been wondering who here could have aided Jessica for years and hid the jewelry pieces, left the notes and trinkets for you, and spelled them. You have your answer. It must be Adelaide. There must be a time or a day, or even just one day a month...something...that releases her for a limited time, so she could have performed such feats. And tend to that bush. Indeed, her blood feeds the poppet, which in turn must mean it keeps Charles alive...or spelled in some way which aids him."

That explains how Wicked could be in my Jeep and a few

of the other incredible feats she had managed over these last few months. I was just astounded in all this time I hadn't seen this transpire. I wondered how no one else managed to discover this all these years and counting.

"Will we never know the truth?" I wondered.

"Donna is the only one left with those answers. With Deanna dead at her hand, we have to get to her. We cannot let the Council raze the prison and destroy her before we get those answers!" Aunt Iona cried out. "Owen, please...you must stop this."

My Uncle Owen put his arm around his wife's shoulders with reassurances he would speak to the Council members and stall any attack on the prison. Olivia agreed.

Andrea and Flora began clearing off the plates and removing the pizza boxes while the rest of us sat in silent contemplation.

I was about to get up and help them, but Olivia stood up and announced she needed to leave. "I want to go look something up and will call you, Adriana, when I have more information. I have some suspicions, but...no. It can wait until I verify what I suspect. Plus, I am weary. I've been feeling under the weather lately, and Hortense Winters has promised me a tisane to set me straight. I'm heading there now and will speak with you tomorrow."

After Olivia departed, we had all assembled back around the dining room table, and I had put on a pot of coffee. With so much information floating around, not to mention the news that had us reeling, we needed time to process. We were a somber bunch staring into our coffee mugs.

That is, we were until Edith chose that moment to fly through the wall and come straight at me.

"Edith! Why are you crashing through walls, woman! Have you no decency!" Adriana groused. She was taken aback by the appearance of my resident ghost and flapped her hands, shooing her away.

"He's coming!" Edith screamed.

"Who is coming? What is wrong with you?" Adriana jumped and pinned our ghost with a heated look. "Stop shouting! I don't understand what you are saying."

"He's coming! Harley. He's on his way here!"

We just went from sordid tales of the past to a full-on zombie attack in less than thirty minutes, and I, for one, had just about had enough.

"That does it. I am not going to deal with one more distraction! If Harley has come back to life and is coming for me, bring it on. I'm ready to rumble!"

CHAPTER 16

*R*eady to rumble? Really? It sounded better in my head than it did when I shouted it out, and everyone effectively ignored me.

"What? How can that be?" Adriana mumbled.

My relatives and friends, who were well aware of my ghost problem, and none of which assumed Adriana and I were sitting there talking to the air around us, had quieted and were awaiting an explanation. This one was going to produce quite the hailstorm.

"Edith is here, and she said Harley is heading this way."

The room exploded with shouting and mayhem. That's better. Now maybe they'd listen to me.

"Edith claims she went on a fact-finding mission when she heard the news that Harley's body went missing. What she found instead was one Harley Jacobs, wrapped in a linen cloth, more than likely naked underneath, wandering around the outskirts of town and heading toward his farm."

Jake immediately went to call the Jacobs and warn them that something utterly incredible was afoot.

We put a call in for Brian, and it went directly to his

voicemail. Then we called the sheriff's office but had to tread softly as the dispatcher is known to be one of the biggest gossips around, and we did not want word of this to get out until we knew what was up. The last thing we needed was half the town in a panic, convinced the zombie apocalypse was here, and the other half ready to let loose a crap-ton of combat magic.

Everyone began running around and talking at the same time—disorganized chaos at its best.

I wasn't sure why everyone was in such a panic and cried out, "Hey! What gives? We've got this... it's just Harley come back from the dead. We can take him out, right? What is zombie protocol around here?"

"Zombies!" Andrea screeched.

"Oh! Oh my! What will we do?" Cousin Flora was wringing her hands and crying.

"Zombie protocol? Zombie *protocol*! There is no such thing as zombies!" Adriana exclaimed.

I, for once, felt a small sense of satisfaction that finally, my family was freaked out by the paranormal. Let's face it. I had been the one to be gobsmacked with witches, sirens, ghosts, and now a vampire, even if his name was as incongruous as Mortimer Snodgrass. This zombie problem seemed old hat to me.

"Do you people not watch television? What's wrong with all of you? This will be easy. It's not like Harley is leading a hoard. It's one zombie against a bevy of witches. He doesn't stand a chance. Um, hello?"

The sheer number of times Andrea alone had run past me in full meltdown mode had put me in a snit. Lorcan was going around locking windows and doors and trying to barricade them with my chairs. As he was heading to the front door, Brian entered, and everyone began shouting at him. I thought he would make a run for it until the words they were saying sunk in.

"No one seems to know where Yolanda is. We called over to see what the story was regarding the missing body, but no one has seen or heard from her in three days."

Hmm...that means Brian hadn't been with her, and I wondered if that kiss he'd given me was still making her stew. I was smiling on the inside.

Petty, I know. *Sue me.*

This news set everyone off again, and this time Brian joined in on the insanity. Someone managed to step on Wicked, who erupted in self-righteous fury. She began ricocheting around the house, spitting and growling until she landed on the top of the hall credenza, where she glared at anyone who'd pass by.

Flora was on her cell phone crying into it at who I presumed was Sebastiano, her father. I could hear his shouting reply from across the room as Sophia tried to reach up and take the phone out of her hands. Flora was very tall and willowy...Sophia, not so much.

Jake was barking orders at everyone while Uncle Owen and Lorcan continued to secure the windows.

Eileen and Henry, with my Aunt's Iona and Chiara, continued to clean up the food mess we'd made, and they had calmed Andrea down enough by making her hold a garbage bag while they deposited stuff in it. Hey, wait, that was a fork and, oh darn it. I just got that flatware!

Dennis was shouting something about clubs and someone named Lucille while June was crying quietly in the corner, the ghost of Moira making there, there pats on her shoulder. Not that June could feel this.

Adriana started chanting, and I suspected she was setting wards around my house.

They didn't work.

How did I know they didn't work?

Because it was at that very moment, Harley Jacobs walked into my formal rooms via the kitchen with both his parents in tow and asked, "Hey folks. I'm back. What the hell is going on around here?"

The only sound for a good minute was Henry Reid's dentures hitting the floor.

* * *

WHAT DO you mean you weren't dead? I saw you. You were positively dead. I would swear my reputation on it," asked Brian, with an amazement-tinged voice.

"I was paralyzed, not dead. The last thing I remember is picking up a hitchhiker...some straggly looking woman who said she lost her job at the chicken plant in Jefferson and needed a ride home to Hiawassee. I told her I could take her as far as Sweet Briar, and she agreed.

I was sipping a soda, and the next thing I know, she asked if I'd stop in the gas station so she could get herself a drink as well. I did since I needed to fill my tank anyway. I pulled in and parked, and then I couldn't move no more. I think she poured some stuff in my drink when I wasn't looking. She left the bottle on my chest. I could see her do it. I just couldn't move."

"Jessamine. The Algonquin tribes in the Carolina's used to paralyze their rivals and then torture them to death. Huh. You mentioned the jessamine, Brian, but I never put two and two together to think he might only be paralyzed and not dead." Adriana stated.

And here, I thought Native Americans were peaceful. And when did Brian mention jessamine to Adriana?

"Damn. I should have listened to Shirley. She stated that from all outward appearances, Harley looked frozen but not expired. She couldn't get any vitals on you, but she said you didn't look like a corpse, but more like some wax replica of you. Frozen in time, but still corporeal since nothing pointed to rigor mortis or the normal state a body goes into when dead. When I think on it, your eyes did seem to have fluids, and you didn't have a deathly pallor." Brian began berating himself, "I owe Shirley an apology."

"But, what about Yolanda? She showed up. Didn't she pronounce him dead?" I asked and could feel Lorcan's eyes boring into the back of my head since this reminded him that Yolanda's arrival followed on the heels of that kiss Brian gave me. Get over it already, buster!

"I don't know. Yolanda was, uh...upset. She called the time for her assistant to scribble down but wasn't in a mood to be thorough in her examination. I guess she went through the motions without really taking a gander at Harley here. I assume she tested the bottle but obviously didn't perform an autopsy which is good for you, Harley."

Eek.

"I didn't want anyone cutting up my boy," stated Mrs. Jacobs, primly, "we didn't want one."

"But surely, she would have examined him...unless...has she been missing all this time? Maybe something has happened to her?" I asked.

Brian looked sheepish, and I realized he hadn't seen her since that day so that he couldn't comment one way or the other as to her actions. Interesting.

"I woke up in that cold room all laid out and nekked. All I could gather up was a sheet, and I didn't wait for daylight to come. I snuck out of that morgue and ran like the dickens through the woods up I-985, trying to stay hidden from sight. Thankfully the entire route up to this part of the state has woods along the highway, or I don't know what I would have done. You see...I didn't know what happened to land me in no morgue. So I thought it prudent to get home to the farm and see what was up before I made my presence known."

"Scared the snot out of me he did." Mr. Jacobs beamed at us, and I suspected he'd rather have the snot scared out of him and have his son back rather than the alternative.

Everyone realized at precisely the same instant that we no longer had a murder case on our hands but still had a lunatic straggly-looking woman on the loose that poisoned Harley for no apparent reason.

"Could it have been Donna?" I asked aloud, but Harley was already shaking his head no at my suggestion.

"I'd know her anywhere...even if she got scrawny from being in prison. It weren't her."

Brian was speaking softly on the phone, and when he hung up, he addressed the room. "My mom is on her way over with Samantha and Rowan. I believe the girl has some-thing to add to this crazy mess."

Now what?

Sophia and Flora took their leave with our promise to update them on any new information to come to light. I don't think Sebastiano was willing to sit around while they stayed with 'that family.' I couldn't blame the guy.

Eileen and Henry, along with Dennis and June, also departed. Henry with teeth intact after rinsing them off in my kitchen sink. They knew the news would travel fast once things settled down. Following them out the door was Uncle Owen, who had to follow up with Council business.

Harley and his grateful parents went home to their farm.

That left me, Lorcan. Adriana, Andrea, Jake, Aunt Iona, and Brian. We sat around the den with coffee and a tray of tea cakes I'd set out. Edith and Moira were here as well, which is how Rita, Samantha, and Rowan found us.

"Have you heard the rumors going around town? That

there is a zombie outbreak?" Rita asked as she was welcomed in by Lorcan, who'd opened the door.

"Oh, I am sure there are tons of rumors going around, but all of them are flat out wrong." Adriana stated, "unless, of course, they happen to be about Harley being alive and well, and recovering from being poisoned enough that he became paralyzed," she finished.

Rita and Samantha stopped short, but Rowan's legs buckled, and if it weren't for quick thinking on Lorcan's part, she might have passed out cold on the floor.

"Here, now. We can't have that. You ok?" He smiled at Rowan, and the poor girl blushed deeply, nodding yes. He settled them into the den with us, and I couldn't help but notice that Rowan sat across from Lorcan and gazed at him in wonder. Oh no. Not another male fixation! I was not about to have her get re-possessed and try to kill me so she could move in on my man. I squinted at her, and Lorcan noticed, giving me a wink and a smile.

I couldn't help but smile back.

This time it was Rowan who squinted.

"Ok, mom...Samantha. What information do you have for us, Rowan?" Brian asked as he came back into the room fresh off another phone call, this one to the sheriff.

Rowan looked down at the ground and whispered, "I don't want to get locked away again."

"Darling. No one made you a prisoner, not really. You went to the hospital. Weren't the Clerics nice? They treated you well."

Rowan nodded but shrunk a little bit more. You couldn't help feeling sorry for her. At least until Lorcan placed his hand on her knee, giving it a shake so she looked up at him, and he won a smile from the besotted teen. Grr.

I know he was hitting her with his empath talent to calm her down and allow her to speak with ease, but I couldn't stop pettiness I never knew I had in me from rearing its ugly head. What was I? In junior high school?

Shaking my head to clear it, I addressed the girl. "Rowan, do you know about what has been happening lately? Something that could help us?"

Rowan shrugged, then sighed audibly.

"I know what happened to that basket...the box, um...in Mr. Jacobs barn."

I had to think a minute about what she was saying then it dawned on me.

"You mean when he said someone stole something out of it? And he accused you of doing so? You told us all you knew about that. Or were you holding something back?"

She nodded yes yet again.

"Only I didn't take it. I watched Harley open the box, and a big smile spread across his face. Then he reached in and touched something that looked like a crown, or no, more like what a fairy princess might wear on her head, some jeweled headpiece. The minute he picked it up, his face went slack, and there was a big popping sound. Then the piece of jewelry began to glow and slowly vanished. I ran out of there, and the next time I saw him, he accused me of stealing something out of the box, but when I asked him what it was, he couldn't remember. So, I knew it must mean dark magic was at play. I wanted no part of it. That's why I didn't tell you the entire story." Rowan stopped talking and ducked her head like she expected us to explode.

We didn't disappoint.

Everyone began firing questions at the teenager, but I fixed my eyes on Adriana, who did the same with me, then nodded. It had to be the circlet that belonged to my set. This means Deanna Fredricks had it among some of her possessions, and Harley had kept them as mementos. But why did it vanish? What dark magic is afoot?

More importantly, what did we need to do about it?

* * *

AFTER EVERYONE HAD LEFT for the evening, I found myself sitting alone in the living room with my fireplace burning embers. Wicked, for once, was curled up on my lap. Well, alone in the sense that besides the cat, I was the only one breathing. Edith and Great Aunt Moira were keeping me company.

"Aunt Moira. How come Olivia could see you, but my great-grandmother doesn't seem to be able to? She sees Edith just fine."

Moira put her ghostly knitting down. Where it wound up, I wasn't entirely sure because it just disappeared from view. Then she turned to give me a sympathetic smile and her full attention.

"Och! I dinnae ken these things, dearie. I just know not tae worry aboot it too much. Yer granny and I were verra close. Even closer than Maggie was with her. Got on like two peas in a pod, we did."

"Yet she can't seem to see you now, so you mustn't be as important as you'd like to believe," sniffed Edith meanly.

"Haud yer wheesht! You silly gurl. Annie and I were besties. Stop being such a bampot."

Ok, then.

"Edith, what is your beef with my aunt here."

"Don't pay her no mind. If she wants tae be nasty, it's no skin off me back. I wouldnae be tellin' Annie aboot me though. Something is blocking her sight. I dinnae want tae bring her any more sorrow."

I smiled at my aunt but turned to Edith once more. "That still doesn't excuse Edith's behavior toward you. Seriously, Edith...what gives?"

"What gives is I've been trying to be helpful all these weeks, and I keep getting dismissed like I'm some unimportant pest instead of a friend."

I didn't have the heart to remind her we weren't exactly friends when she was alive; that seemed a bit cruel.

"Edith, while I appreciate all the help you have been giving me as of late, I..."

"And I can help you get through the lower levels of the library if we can just figure out how to get to wherever the spell is. I've been there. I know what to expect! Plus, she's here a few days, and you seem to like her better than me."

"Edith. I understand completely. And you are wrong...I am equally, um...incredulous to have two, uh...otherworldly guests. But forget about that for a minute. As to the forbidden library conundrum, without knowing where the bit of passage torn out of that spellbook wound up, we have no reason to go down there in the first place!"

As I said this, Wicked came into the room, then stopped when she spied the two ghosts keeping me company. She walked by Moira without a backward glance but puffed and hissed at Edith.

"Ok, what gives? Wicked used to be fine with you. Now suddenly, she hates the very sight of you, Edith. Did you do something to her?"

Edith looked down and her hands and squirmed a bit. "I think Adelaide can hear me. I think she is aware, and the cat reacts based on how your aunt feels about a situation."

"Ok, but so? Why would she react to you this way?"

"I think she realizes I left something out when I told you about my previous trip to the forbidden area of the library."

Are you kidding me?

What's with people holding back the complete truth?

"Oh, Edith! Why? What didn't you tell us?"

Edith looked miserable, and even I felt sorry for her. I

gave her time to answer, though, and didn't prod her any more than my initial question, figuring she'd answer in due time.

I wasn't wrong in my assumption.

"What I didn't tell you was the Book of Ancients that had been tampered with and had the passage torn out of it had trace spells which led Olivia to discover Deanna as the culprit."

"Yes, we know this...Olivia went over this with us. What aren't you saying?"

"The little totem I pulled out of my pocket in that cupboard, the one Olivia crafted as a key, was a tiny black cat with green eyes. When I touched it, I could see a path to a small hidden room just off the main room where the book lies.

When I went to inspect it, I saw a glass dome with the ripped-out pages inside. In front of the dome was a velvet draped rectangle with a circle impression, almost like it needed something to be placed in front of it so the glass would open and I could take the pages out. I think what that means is we need some sort of key. But, even with the key, an inscription written down on a plaque nearby stated the I'd need to utter the correct spell, or the lock would not open. I'm afraid, even if I can lead you to the exact spot, without the key and spell, you'll never get that parchment out."

Just great. Why did there always seem to be roadblock after roadblock?

"Edith, why would you keep this to yourself?"

Again, looking woebegone and ashamed, my ghostly visitor whispered out a remorseful reply, "I wanted to feel important and hoped you'd keep asking me for help. I thought, if I held this as my trump card when the time came, you'd feel like you needed me enough to be nice to me, and you'd like me better if I saved the day. I was going to say something. I promise you I was!"

Oh, Edith.

Sighing, I shook my head and wished I could at least reach out and pat her hand, knowing it would be fruitless. I couldn't seem to touch ghosts, unlike my cousin in North Carolina.

"Well, it doesn't matter much, does it? Because we have no clue what the key is, nor which spell would unlock that dome."

Moira clapped her hands softly to get our attention. "Ladies, haud on now...dinnae worry. I think I have this figured oot. I think I ken what the key could be. You heard it last night. The circlet. It vanished when auld Harley touched it, and if it be the one made by Maggie's father-in-law, Regie's father, it has the key pattern on it. The imprint is a circle shape ye said, the circlet be the key!"

Could be. That very well could be the case. But without a spell to recite, we'd still have no way to get those papers. Not to mention the fact that the circlet vanished, and we had no idea where it disappeared to.

a few days had passed, and we seemed to be at the mercy of the Witch Council. Word had spread far and wide about Harley's miracle recovery. Although how you can recover from death was beyond me. I kept correcting everyone and explaining the paralysis, but folks just seemed to prefer the death thing.

Uncle Owen, Aunt Chiara, and Olivia had argued well the case for not blasting the prison to Kingdom Come. Although, in Olivia's case, she'd done her arguing from home because she had, in fact, come down with some kind of bug.

So far, it looked like they had enough weight to sway the votes to our side.

We would be weeks out in planning our attack on the lower levels and trying to wrest the control away from Donna, recapture her, and dismantle her army. I'd wondered how they were getting food and water and other supplies until it was made known to me that any piddling witch could make a loaf of bread and a cup of water appear out of thin air as long as they kept crumbs and a few drips from a previous meal. That was a handy trick I still needed to learn.

Visions of regenerating cannoli had me drooling. Not to mention I wouldn't have to cook as often nor slave over a hot stove as long. It was all very Bewitched, and I wanted more of it, what an about-face from when I first discovered my witchy abilities.

I felt deflated after the uproar over these last few days and found myself wandering around the town square. The comforting sounds of the usual morning routines soothed my nerves.

Gordy Polk was out and about picking up the garbage in his prize truck, and he gave a toot of the horn as he passed Joe's Diner. Sheila, his wife, waved a menu at him as she seated folks looking for a good breakfast.

June was sweeping the front walk and waved at me as I strolled by on the village green. I walked past the gazebo and noticed it was all decked out in Valentine décor, and I belatedly realized the holiday was fast approaching. I wondered what it would mean for Lorcan and me. Too soon to celebrate like an official couple and get a small gift? I hadn't a clue.

Becky was arranging her storefront, and I could see hearts in the window and suspected all the titles would have something to do with romance.

Even the Winters Sisters were busy bustling around the front of the tea shop. I could see a supplier bringing in orders and Hermione and Hortense giving directions while still trying to take care of customers.

I decided to head over to my Uncle Stephen's café and get my breakfast there. I hadn't seen much of him or his son Steve Junior lately. They were busy this time of year and had avoided the family drama, waiting to be updated when they arrived home.

Walking into Enchanté Café, I almost did an about-face and walked right back out again when I spied Nora at a table just inside the entrance. She looked up at the same instant I walked in, so there was no escape. I chose to ignore her and strolled past where she was seated with barely a glance, heading to the counter to await service.

I didn't have long to wait. Steve Junior swept in all smiles and started his flirting campaign in earnest.

"I thought I heard butterflies sighing. How did I know I'd find you gracing the café with your beauty?"

"Good morning to you as well, Stevie. What tasty treat is on the menu today?"

"If you'd just take a nibble out of me, you'd realize there is nothing in this shop sweeter, except maybe yourself."

Rolling my eyes and giggling, I ordered a cheese danish and a cappuccino. I turned and sat at the table closest to the counter and was there for less than the time it took for me to bite into my danish and swallow when I felt Nora approach. I didn't even have to look up to know she was waiting for me to notice her.

"What?"

I didn't feel like using the usual social graces.

Nora widened her eyes, then squinted as if she was gearing up for a fight, but then she deflated.

"May I take a seat?"

"What, here? With me?"

I knew I was snarky, but I couldn't help myself. I do snark so well.

Ignoring my jibe, Nora took the seat across from me and signaled to Steve that she'd like another coffee.

"Talk, Nora. I don't feel like playing any games. What do you want?"

"I think I can help you...um, with your Adelaide problem," whispering quietly, Nora glanced around to see if anyone might overhear.

I scrutinized her face trying to ascertain whether or not

this was some elaborate trick only someone as insufferable as my cousin Nora would enact. Most disturbing to discover, I couldn't find even a hint of malice in her demeanor. Not even the slightest.

"Before you tell me anything further, I need to know why you are offering help, Nora. You can understand why I am hesitant even to hear what you have to say."

Nora sat back, and I could feel her fighting the usual sarcastic vitriol that usually came bubbling to the surface where I was concerned.

"Look. I saw my mother the other day. I happened to run into her, and she looks awful. I've heard from Brian what is going on in the family—especially regarding Adelaide. The turn of events has everyone trying to free her from the spell. I think I have something that might help."

"First, tell me why you wanted this ring so badly."

I noticed Nora glancing at it surreptitiously ever since sitting at my table and knew she wanted is desperate enough to have spearheaded the coup attempt with Edith before Edith died at the hands of Rowan.

"Moreover, do you know who is behind the possession of Rowan Nightingale? Do you have any idea who is trying to destroy this family and might be aiding and abetting Donna?"

"I don't. No. You have to believe me! I have no idea what happened to Rowan, and I am devastated over Edith. She really was my best friend." Nora looked crestfallen at having to relive what had happened at Nichols Pond, so I didn't think she was lying.

"I wanted the ring because I want the power it holds. It's as simple as that. I am a Croy too. I don't know why it shouldn't come to me. You were never here. I spent my entire life having to hear about you. But I never left. I was here all along. Why shouldn't it come to me?"

I wasn't going to get into it with Nora over this. She had her opinions. I had mine. Forget the fact that I'd had no choice about leaving nor over what the three most influential people in my life, at that time, had decided. It was out of my hands.

"Tell me. What do you have?"

"I know where the passage torn out of the spellbook you have been seeking is, the glass dome it's locked in. I know how to find the circlet that I suspect you've heard about by now, and I think I know the dark magic needed to open the case holding the paper. You'll need the circlet and the dark magic spell if you expect to reverse the spell on Adelaide."

Well, if there was one thing I thought I'd ever hear come out of Nora's mouth, that wasn't it.

* * *

THAT'S how I found myself in the library once again. This time Nora accompanied Adriana, Susanne Washington, and me. It was an odd group, I'll admit. My friend, and current head librarian, Martha Mosely, raised her eyes when she spied Nora following me into the meeting room. I gave her a shrug and a look that said, yeah, right?

I had been neglecting poor Martha as of late. She and Becky had tried to start a book club with Andrea and me, but we never seemed to have the time. Something I hoped to reconcile after I solved this little mystery. Keisha Holcomb had heard about it and was keen, so we may start one up— once our lives got semi-normal, that is.

We had heard from Brian and Sheriff Glen that Yolanda was still missing, and they suspected foul play of some sort as all the paperwork regarding Harley was gone. Harley's case had been closed, however, because, well, he was alive. They followed up on some leads regarding the 'scraggly-looking female' that Harley had picked up in his truck. Reports in Clayton had some vagrants in the area, and one of the descriptions matched what Harley could recollect of the woman, which wasn't much. It was a long shot, but what else could they do?

As we sat around the table and Martha excused herself, closing the door to the room to give us some privacy, all eyes turned to Nora, and Adriana spoke first. "Ok, what do you have for us?"

"I've been doing a lot of research on this, family lore and looking into old tomes that had historical data on others of our kind who had similar objects of power made. I know the circlet will always be available to the one who has the rest of the pieces of the set or who has commanded it prior. That means if Lily wants it, it should appear in some way. I suspect she needs to place her hands on the glass, and it will just appear." I could see Adriana nodding her agreement with this statement as I drummed my fingers on the table, deep in thought.

"Hold on. Why were the items separated, do you think? The set of jewelry. Perhaps someone was trying to take them from Adelaide?"

"No. I don't think so. I think Adelaide hid them herself and put spells on them. That's why the circlet disappeared when Harley handled it. Deanna may have found it among her things but probably didn't realize what it was at the time."

"Then why didn't it do the same when I found the ring? Put it on?" I asked.

Adriana smiled at me but didn't say anything. I thought about it a moment, then stated, "Because Adelaide wanted me to have them."

It made sense.

"Ok, so now what? Do I just go down into the forbidden library again and chant this dark spell? I don't know if I feel comfortable speaking dark magic that I shouldn't utter. What will the consequences be?"

No one had an answer to that.

"There is going to be a price to pay. There always is when one executes dark magic," intoned Susanne in a somber voice.

That's precisely what Tari Vanderzee stated.

"All that is well and good, but without the dark spell to chant, none of this will work anyway. So, Nora, do you have it?" I asked.

"I have it. I had already decided to help you the other day when I saw you driving by. I knew you'd need to know about the circlet, all the jewelry, for a long time now, and decided to share that with you, if only for my mother's sake."

Adriana was reaching into her purse and pulled out a cell phone. My great-grandmother owned a cell phone? I didn't have time to comment because she was already speaking into it.

"Brian. Adriana. Can you text me that photo you took of the poppet? I need that inscription. No, I can't tell you why. I am busy at the library helping Lily. Just send it." She hung up, with Brian making squawking sounds we could easily hear as she disconnected the call. Adriana then drummed her fingers across the table as I had been doing. Suddenly we heard a 'ding.' It looks like Brian came through with that photo.

Adriana read the words aloud once more so we could all hear it:

Words are no matter;

only glass will blood shatter
Draught of elderberry,
mixed with strands of heir
Take this poppet to open the lair
Curse reversed, and all is well
The one who is left standing...
...is sacrificed to Hell.

"USELESS, unless we can figure out what it means." I grumped. "Ominous sounding, too, like the victor loses anyway and gets cast into hell?"

I reached out for the phone and read through the saying one more time.

"How am I going to get through to the room with the book, anyway? Do you know how I can escape these Sentinels?"

"I've tried to reach Olivia again to verify what potion she made to make Edith invisible to the guardians, but she is too sick to pick up her phone. You'd think a grown witch would be able to heed the warning signs and stave off getting ill by proactively getting spelled potions into her system. I mean, really!"

"So that's it then. We need to wait for Olivia to get better."

"No, we do not need Olivia to get better. I said I called to verify, not that I didn't know what she used. I have a pretty good idea. And it correlates with this riddle which I find highly interesting."

I looked at Adriana in shock, as did Nora.

"What do you mean? It's in this riddle?"

"It is."

We waited for Ariana to elaborate, but instead, she pulled a small vial out of her bag and passed it over to me.

"I made this yesterday. I believe it will do the trick."

"Wait. How can you know that? Explain."

I folded my arms and jutted out my lip, stubbornly refusing even remotely to consider drinking something my great-grandmother brewed without further enlightenment.

"Elderberries. I made a potion using elderberries, as the riddle says. It's common knowledge for cloaking spells to use elderberries."

Nora looked confused as well. "But you only recently saw the riddle. How did you interpret it to be similar to what Olivia used for Edith? And how do you know you have all the ingredients needed?"

"Because I've been around a lot longer than you two witchlings, and I already had a key component. Read the puzzle. Draught of elderberry." Adriana stated smugly.

"Yes...but it goes on to a misspelled error. Strand of heir? That should be hair."

"Correct...but it has a double meaning."

"Double...I don't understand."

"It needs hair from an heir to work...and I just so happened to have your hair and used it in the spell to create this potion."

"No, you didn't."

"Yes, I did."

"You did not!"

"Yeppers!"

"Ladies! Please. Can we move this along? My sciatica is acting up, and I can't sit around here listening to you squabble much longer!" Susanne scolded the two of us.

"I did. As a matter of fact, it was the last time the two of us were sitting in this very library. You came rushing in, late for our meeting, and you had that paper clip stuck on your head. When you pulled it out, some strands of your hair came with it. You tossed it down on the table, and I swiped it off and saved it in my purse—just in case I'd ever need it."

I sat there, mouth agape, incredulous that this imp in granny clothing would keep my DNA and use it for nefarious purposes. Then again, this is the woman who sliced my hand open and used me as a sacrifice, so I didn't know why I should be so shocked.

"And I was *not* late."

"So, you say."

All eyes turned once again to the vial and then to me as I gently took it and placed it in my bag.

"It says blood will shatter the glass....and there is a potion...but there are no words needed—only a sacrifice. Someone's going to hell, whoever remains standing. But what does it mean? How will I know what to do?"

For the first time, I saw the worry in my great-grand-mother's eyes and something that troubled me more than anything else. Her eyes held another emotion—fear.

"Am I going to have to die to free my mother from this curse? Will getting the spell mean I am the last one standing, and I, what? Die and go to this hell mentioned?"

"Not if I can help it, cara," replied Adriana softly.

"I have one more thing." Nora piped up suddenly, and I turned to her in suspicion. If she noticed, she didn't let on that she did.

"Edith found a small saying written on some papers of Adelaide's we found in a box my mom had kept. It's what started this entire plan of ours to get the sweet briar rose jewelry. It's a simple spell, but I think it might work in this case." Nora slipped a piece of paper over to the middle of the table then sat back.

Adriana looked at the paper but didn't touch it. She slapped at my hand when I reached out for it, surprising Susanne and me.

"That's emanating some dark magic, Nora. Very dark magic. Yet it is in Adelaide's handwriting. She was always such a talented dark witch, so much promise. But this? This is foul."

Nora looked at Adriana nodding her head. "But dark magic is needed in this case to break such a vile spell. I think I figured out what happened all those years ago. I think Adelaide was working on a dark magic spell, and Deanna found it. Then she used it on Adelaide. It's the only thing that makes sense. Adelaide brought about her own destruction, albeit inadvertently, and without the knowledge that Deanna had discovered what she had created."

Even as Nora told us this story, I knew it was the truth. I could feel it. Donna and Deanna might have Croy in them, but Adelaide was a dark witch. Those two vile sisters only used what power they could glean from familial jewelry, but even with that, they could never have created dark magic such as this. Adelaide, however, could.

What a sad and horrible mess.

I looked at the incantation and knew I only could perform this spell. I was, after all, Adelaide's heir. I read her handwriting, memorizing the words. I wondered at how simple the line she wrote seemed, yet knew the power the words would produce.

"I'm doing this. I will go down there now and end this curse once and for all."

"Oh no, you're not. Not without me along to help you." Lorcan came storming into the room with Brian on his heels.

"Not without me there either. What do you think you are doing, Adriana? She is a new witch. She shouldn't have to go this alone!" Brian protested.

I guessed Brian had put two and two together with the phone call and surprisingly contacted Lorcan. Before me, they were good friends until I caused the rift. I believe the two decided it would be prudent to join forces against any protest I might give.

"What now?" Nora asked.

"Now? Lily enters the Forbidden Library." Adriana declared.

Cue the creepy organ music.

CHAPTER 18

This time I didn't complain about walking three miles to get to the room where Jerry, my Fairy Godfather, resided. He was thrilled to see me again but quickly sobered when he comprehended what I was about to do.

"Darling, you will be perfectly fine. I just know it. You wait and see. I'm *never* wrong."

Susanne waited for me on the other side of the door, the same as before. She drove quickly to the church and headed to the lower level and entrance to the forbidden area.

Nora wanted to come along, but Adriana nixed the idea. I thought she treated Nora a bit harshly, all things considered, but I wasn't about to stick up for a cousin who had given me so much grief and all of it unwarranted. Nora was a big girl. She'd just have to live with her decisions and accept how my great-grandmother felt about allowing her further access.

I did feel I owed her something. I just wasn't sure what as of yet. I stated this to Adriana, amazed at this turn of events as far as Nora went.

"Sometimes keeping your enemies close can have unexpected benefits, Liliana. We'll figure out what to do about Nora. I don't know if having these two Neanderthals along for the ride will alter the spell. I don't think there is enough potion to hide you all from the Sentinels, nor do I think it will last as long if it does cloak you. Which means you have less time to perform the incantation. Maybe I should go in and let the men stay here standing guard."

"No. We go together with Lily, or she stays. It's not up for argument." Lorcan growled. Brian nodded in agreement.

Edith was hovering in the corner, not saying much, but it looked like she was waiting for me to acknowledge her. I had to give it to the ghost—she didn't have to help me. She never had to bother with me or try to coach me through the labyrinth below, yet she offered her aid.

Turning to her, I exclaimed, "I am so glad you are here to help guide me, Edith. I don't think I could do this without you."

If a specter could look more shocked and pleased, I don't know how, but Edith positively radiated unbridled joy before getting serious.

"Ok, then. Lily, you need to remember one thing. Never remove your hand from the right side of the wall. Always take the right path, even if it looks like you should go left. Never. Never, ever, go left. You will get lost."

I nodded to show her I understood, waiting for her to continue.

"I will try to be there with you...but last time I couldn't seem to follow you through the employee bathroom in the library...that's why I came this way, this time. But if I can't follow again, try to remember that more than anything, stay to the right.

Also, if the magic wears off and the Sentinels awaken, I tossed the little totem in that last room before I resurfaced. You are going in reverse, which means that totem will be in the third to last room before you are in the same room as the book."

Huh?

I must have looked confounded because she explained further.

"Look...you are going in this door here and will immediately walk down a flight of stairs, ok? Then you will come to another door. That is the first room. Get through that one until the next door...that's the second room. The next door will lead you to the third room, where the totem should be somewhere on the floor. Then you will be in the room with the book. After that, you need to see if the totem shows you the hidden room like it did me. If you walk into the last door and see the book in front of you, the hidden room is to your right, just beyond a small alcove."

"Hang on a minute. That sounds too easy! What's with the 'keep your hand on the right wall talk? If I just go down some steps and count the doors, why do I need to worry about pathways and getting lost or turned around?"

Edith worried her bottom lip with her teeth. "Because the rooms change as you enter them. They change as you walk through them. Things happen down there, and nothing is the same as the last time you go through. But the doors don't change, so count them and make sure you stay to the right."

"Change? How?"

"I don't know how to explain it...they just...breathe, morph, they change!"

I could hear the soothing sound of the choir practicing far above me, and it calmed my nerves. The room was silent as we absorbed what Edith told me after passing it along to Lorcan and Brian.

"What about the Sentinels? What if they awaken? What do they look like? And how do I get away from them? Can I fight? Use magic?" I was trying to keep on a brave face, but the knowledge of what I was about to attempt was making me hinky. My voice even squeaked a bit.

"I've never seen them, Lily. I only heard them oozing. That's all I can tell you. They sound like nothing you have ever heard—and they ooze. Every step they take sounds as painful to them as it does to your ears for hearing them moan and gnash their teeth. I hope you never have to face them."

Lovely.

I looked around and realized no one in this room had ever seen them. Perfect. No one had any advice on what to do if I should run into these oozing entities. Or...

"Didn't you say Grandfather Antonio had the secret entrance put in the prison...and didn't he put Sentinels in the lower levels to guard it along with Mortimer? Or Mortimer's dad? So, couldn't my great-grandfather tell me about them, or better yet, put in a good word about me, so they leave us alone?"

"It doesn't work that way, Lily. These are creatures that, once activated, become sentient beings that understand only one thing. Find the intruder and remove it by any means. No one can control them. Magic can be used to put them to sleep for a bit or make you invisible. Again, only for a short time. But what is the point of having a forbidden library if it's easy to get in? They made them impossibly dangerous for that reason."

"But what about Mortimer? Surely, he has run into them being the guardian of that gate. Can't he help?"

Adriana gave me a weighted look that spoke volumes, although I wasn't sure what that even meant.

"Mortimer could keep them from you, but I can't get him to help us."

"Why not?"

"Because he sealed the entrance to the prison after I

instructed him to, but he forgot to tell me what he intended to do next and more than likely is sleeping it off somewhere. Vampires tend to sleep for decades." She stated in a quiet voice.

"Can't you call him? I mean, if you need to reach him for something, don't you have his number?"

"Lily. Vampires usually do not go around carrying cell phones! They are Ancients. They tend to stay old-fashioned."

Tell that to Fred and Linda Snodgrass, Mortimer's parents, happily living their retirement days in Boca.

"But how hard could it be to find a sleeping vampire? He's a big, giant vampire. I'm sure someone has seen him crawling into a coffin, or...hey! Call the Soule's. Maybe he showed up at Chester and Hester's funeral parlor looking for a bed."

"No, Lily. Mortimer is part shifter, too, remember? It's more likely he has turned himself into a bucket and is hanging over an old abandoned well somewhere so he can get some rest."

Well...isn't that just great.

"Then it's up to me to get to that dome, shatter the glass if the circlet comes when I call it, and get those passages. Right? Do I read them? This has been such a hodge-podge jumble of theories for so long that I am confused."

Susanne had been sitting quietly but finally cleared her throat. "As gatekeeper, I am allowed to open this gate and let you enter. I also can allow anyone who has permission from the Council to enter, which is rare. So rare, it has only happened nine times since I've been the gatekeeper. Each time the person allowed entry had a totem. Olivia went behind the Council's back with Edith, used a draught, and gave Edith the totem. I say your best bet is to try and find the totem first, then enter the room. If you can't find it, drink the draught amongst the three of you, equal sips to buy time, and try for the passages. Please don't rely on the potion, however...no disrespect, Adriana, but it never works for long. Split among three?"

She smiled at Adriana as if seeking approval.

"Once you reach the dome, the circlet will appear if you place your hands on the glass. Both of your hands. Those domes work sort of like a locker. Ancient witches used to hide their old spells away in them that they didn't want anyone to get their hands on. This one has been used in the same manner.

Place your hands on the glass dome and think of the circlet. It should appear in the indentation and is the first key. Then you need to state the words Adelaide penned, and that dome will shatter. Inside, that piece of parchment holds the reversal spell and something else. It will hold a key of some sort to get you out of the lower levels. Make sure Lorcan and Brian are holding on to you in case you are all whisked out of there in a hurry, ok?"

Oh my. I was getting Harry Potter port key vibes, and I didn't like it one bit. I knew I would be on guard for any evil shenanigans to transpire and remain on high alert even without the Sentinels hunting me.

I had no sooner finished thinking these thoughts when I heard an unholy ruckus way above us in the church. I could hear the choir screaming and jolted along with everyone in the room.

"What the...?"

Brian and Lorcan, along with Susanne, ran from the chamber and started upstairs to find out what was causing the discord. They only reached the top of the stairs and threw open the door for that answer to come strolling in like a foul odor.

"Wicked! What are you doing here?"

"Let me go settle the choir down before they go get Old Cletus and his bloodhound to hunt your cat." Susanne hustled upstairs, and we returned to the room with my inky black furball.

"I think she means to go in there with you," said Adriana.

"What? No way. Nuh-uh. You are staying here, young lady, and that's final."

With that pronouncement made, all I could do was watch in abject horror as Wicked walked over to the entrance to the lower levels and jumped up at the doorknob. Yep...it opened for her, and in she went.

CHAPTER 19

"Can't you control that cat...like, ever?"

Lorcan was in a foul mood, and Brian wasn't too far off. We had shouted up to Susanne, who ran back downstairs and pushed us through the entrance after my cat. Then slammed the door shut before any of us could change our minds. We were now at the bottom of the steps and ready to enter the first door. Thankfully, Edith seemed to be able to enter along with us and was floating beside me.

"OK, everyone needs to hold hands...make a chain. I need to keep my hand on the right wall, but my left needs to, oof!" Lorcan had jostled Brian out of the way and grabbed my left hand. Oh, brother.

Brian took Lorcan's left hand with a sigh. Lorcan kept smirking at him with an eat dirt grin. Edith tried to hold on to Brian's hand, but hers went right through his, and she shrugged. Brian didn't even realize her attempt, although he did shiver once. Then we steadied ourselves as I turned the knob. I wasn't sure what we'd do about Wicked.

Thankfully she waited for us to enter and then patiently sat while we looked around.

My fingertips firmly pressed up to the right wall, I became aware of a distant sound, like water sloshing up against a wall.

"That's the Sentinels, I think they are sleeping, and that sound is them breathing," Edith whispered. Oh, I didn't like this one bit. I nodded and crept forward a few steps, only to have the walls in front of us shift, and a greenish smoke began oozing up from the floor to the ceiling, tendrils wispy and swirling as we moved.

I sensed it before it happened and locked my hand tightly to Lorcan's. "The floor is crumbling away. I don't know what to do!" I stated in a loud whisper. We pitched forward and slid down an incline as the floor seemed to break apart a few inches and sent us down an assembly line of sorts. Once we reached the bottom, the floor turned into dirt, thick, loamy, peat moss-like dirt. If someone told me I was walking on an open grave, I'd believe them—so dank and odiferous was the ground before us.

"Do you hear crickets?" I looked at my friends, and all three of them nodded yes. Wicked seemed to be batting the ground all around her, and I shook my hand loose of Lorcan so he would release it, allowing me to pull my phone out of my pocket. Brian and Lorcan crowded close, and they helped me turn the light on so we could see better. I immediately wished we hadn't. The floor wasn't dirt at all. We were walking on what appeared to be at least three feet deep, pure crickets, and they were jumping. Everywhere. Wicked was having a blast and...

"Stop *eating* them! Ugh! Stupid cat."

I looked up and saw the next door looming.

We hurried as fast as we dared over our undulating floor and, taking a deep breath, opened the door, slipping into the next room. Instantly we knew this room would be very different from the last. First of all, we could easily see because giant torches were lit and brightened the room considerably. Second, the very ground seemed to be made of smoothly sliced crystals that reflected the light from above.

It was akin to walking on fire but without the pain...or flames. The last thing I noticed was the room was a circular shape, and as we followed along the path, the floor led us down in a spiral. We strolled along, and not much else happened, but we hardly let down our guard. The sound of sloshing goo got louder with every step, preventing us from relaxing.

I don't know how long we continued on the path, but my legs were tiring, so I expected we'd been at it for some time. Right when I thought it would be nice to sit for a spell, we leveled off and came to a section with an extended bench. I didn't even ask. I headed straight for it, keeping my hand in place, then skooched the men along in front of me so they could sit to my left while I gratefully took the seat closest to the wall.

That's when the bench decided to take us on a ride. Seriously. We lurched forward, which slammed us back in our seats. Thankfully, Wicked had jumped onto Lorcan's lap, so she wasn't left behind.

"This feels like a ride in a funhouse. A dark, scary one." The guys nodded, and we realized there was no longer a wall for me to hold. Instead, we kept our hands together with a protective hold on Wicked. The bench was moving fast!

"Hang on tight...it looks like we are going to crash through the next door!" Brian whispered harshly; his voice slightly panicked.

"Quick...drink the potion...we are heading into the third room! Hurry." Fumbling, I pulled the bottle out of my pocket and handed it to Lorcan, who took a sip, then passed it to Brian, who did the same. But before they could hand it back to me, we realized the door was upon us.

I wanted to close my eyes, but instead, we braced for the crash that never happened. As we made our rapid approach, the doors opened, and we flew into the next room. The bench stopped short and pitched us forward onto the floor, then backed up the way it had come with the doors closing softly in their wake.

Horror-filled, I realized my hands were now in front of me, palms flat on the floor. I looked around but couldn't see any walls, just inky blackness. I whimpered a little as I realized we seemed to be in a chamber that lacked not only walls but a ceiling as well. What was worse, the sloshing goopy breathing had risen in crescendo. It felt like we were surrounded.

"We need to look for the totem. This is the third room, right, Edith? Edith?"

No Edith.

I turned around. No Lorcan or Brian either.

Ohmygosh! *OH. MY.GOSH!*

The sound of the sloshing changed to one of grumbling and growling. Then I heard it, the unmistakable sound of oozing and popping and gnashing of teeth. Holy sweet mother of all things scary! The Sentinels were coming!

I clambered to my feet and wasn't sure if I was thrilled or concerned to find Wicked sitting quietly blinking up at me, a look of utter boredom on her whiskered face.

"Now what?" I asked her.

"Mreow!"

"You know that doesn't help, right? I can't speak cat."

She gave me one more lazy blink then walked a few feet away from me, sniffing at something on the ground. Following her, I bent over and saw it was the cat totem with green eyes.

"Meroow?"

"Good job, Wicked! We needed this!"

As I reached down to grab onto it, the floor tilted, and my legs kicked out from under me. I could hear my toe connect with the tiny figure and heard it ping across the room. Oh no! No, no, no! I flew across the floor with Wicked firmly attached to my head, her front paws in my hair and her back ones digging into the flesh on my shoulders. Making a pathetic *eep* sound, I hit the wall—see...there was one—then dropped to the floor and began scrambling around looking for the totem.

I couldn't figure out the next noise that hit my ears, but it sounded like a cat whose tail got caught in a grinder. Then I realized it was the cat on my head in full freak-out mode, so I looked up to see why she sounded like death warmed over.

I was now staring at death warmed over.

No, really.

Edith said she'd never seen the Sentinels but that they sounded like oozing goo. What I was now gawping at totally explained the noise. The thing before me had eyes and a face, and a human-like form. However, that's where the similarities ended. It was big. Bigger than Mortimer Snodgrass, the vampire, and that was massive! Where skin should be, however, was something that would surely give me nightmares for the rest of my life, should I survive this—and I didn't like my odds. The surface of this creature was glowing, grayish, wet, snot-like goop.

If that weren't horrible enough, every few seconds, a tiny human shape would shoot up and out away from the monster, arms reaching high above its tiny head. It was as if trying to break through the wet skin to freedom, only to get sucked back into the community of oozing mass. But it wasn't just one tiny humanoid form vying for release. It was hundreds. All were making the same 'plop, plop, fizz' noise that would be hysterical in an Alka-Seltzer commercial if the creature in front of me weren't so dreadful.

"Mmph." I think I was trying to call out to my mother, either one of them. I tried backing up, but I was already pressed up against the wall.

Wicked had shot off my head and was standing in front of me, puffed up to epic proportions, and growling like a fierce warrior kitty. I was so proud of her. But terrorized at the thought of this thing snatching her up and eating her whole.

Oh, yeah, *teeth.*

It didn't have a normal mouth with long, sharp, greenish-yellow teeth. No. It had three mouths with long, sharp green-ish-yellow teeth, all of which were gnashing and spitting and freaking me out. However, a second equally gruesome beast rose behind the first and roared if that wasn't horrific enough. That was the only definition I could come up with in my near-frozen state. Sliding to the ground, I felt tears streaming down my face, yet I was determined not to give up without a fight. I'd die trying to save my fearless cat.

Before I could unleash my magic on the vile creatures, Wicked darted to my right and caught the attention of the Sentinels, who zeroed in on her like the hunters they are. I screamed out a warning and slid forward, waiting in fasci-nated horror as I saw the first monster raise up a massive fist to smash down on my helpless feline. But then my hand connected with the totem.

Bam! Just like that, the two guardians shrunk down to a more normal height of around seven feet, if I had to guess, turned on their squishy heels, and ambled up the corridor they'd come down, sliding into a puddle of liquid jelly-like slop.

The minute they turned, a doorway to my right gave off a faint white glow, so I scooped up my cat and crept-walked forward into that passageway. The faint, unearthly glow gave me just enough light to see a few steps in front of where I was going. Next, I came upon three arches. Two were brightly lit beyond, but the third, the one on the far right, was obscured completely.

Sigh.

"Why am I not surprised?" Follow the right path. Follow the right path!

Heading into the darkness, I once again felt a wall, and kept my hand brushing along its surface, occasionally peering behind me to make sure those nasty boogers weren't coming up from behind. The wall was cool to the touch, like marble or limestone.

I walked along, alone except for my feline companion, wondering what happened to my three friends. Part of me almost expected this to be the case...knowing no matter what they'd said, I'd have to face this alone. I was deep in thought and almost cried out in alarm when I just about smacked into the last door.

Placing my left hand up against it, I whispered, "Here goes nothing," and watched as it slowly opened before me.

The room beyond was awash in a soft white glow around the edges. I couldn't see what was making the light, but I was grateful for it, nonetheless. I saw the book on a table in front of me. Turning to my right, I peered over to where the alcove should be and was elated to not only see the opening but the glass dome beyond.

Barely giving the ancient book another glance, I walked through the alcove and approached the glass dome.

It was making a slight humming noise, and I wasted no time placing my hands on its smooth round surface and visualizing the circlet as Edith described to me. I heard an imperceptible increase in the volume of the humming noise and felt a frisson in the air. When I looked down, the circlet was sitting snugly in the velvet impression that was just vacant. It looked like it had fused into the indentation that held it on the podium.

Circlet. Check.

Next, I imagined the scrap of paper that held my mother's elegant cursive script and spoke the words she had penned:

As I am a Dark Witch bred from Dark Witches,
I call upon ancestor or heir,
release thy curse, and with blood and tears,
this shall fulfill the price of evil.
Cast one soul into the labyrinth,
and free me from my bondage.
The sacrifice will satisfy the emolument,
forever lost to Time.

Recite spell. Check.

I waited for just about the count of ten when Wicked began to shake, falling to her side.

"Oh, no! No. Don't you dare die. Please! Take me. I'm the sacrifice. Not my brave little girl!" I was crying and trying to comfort my cat when a bright light all but blinded me, tossing me backward with force like the wind from a hellish storm. The entire room shuddered. A high-pitched whine was relentlessly broadcasting, and I held my hands to my ears, eyes squeezed shut and huddled in place.

Then just like that, silence.

When the light faded, the sight before me had me astounded, tears falling anew, only these were tears of happiness.

"Hello, Lily. I'm Adelaide...your mother." I quickly let my eyes roam over the woman standing before me, and I cried out in ecstatic joy when I saw my Wicked little black cat sitting at Adelaide's feet, gazing up at my mother in worship.

My mother.

Just...*wow.*

"I don't even know what to say."

"Understandable. I knew you'd free me, though. I knew you had it in you, the ability to wear those jewelry pieces and absorb the power within them."

"You did? I mean, it took some time. I can't believe you are really here. I'm so sorry all this happened to our family, to you. You look so pale. Do you feel OK? What happened all those years ago?"

"Oh, darling. I'm the one who is sorry for everything. I am tired. The magic that held me was foul. I can explain everything, I hope. But for now? I am so thrilled to be standing here and looking at my beautiful girl."

"Oh, how sweet. Get it? Sweet? Not really. I think it's disgusting. But I am thrilled to have both Croy women in my sights."

No way. I refused to believe the voice I was hearing would manifest into the hated face of my enemy. But sure enough, when I turned around, there stood Yolanda Serrano. And she was holding a ball of magic in the palm of her hand. This was not good.

"Yolanda. What are you doing here? How did you get here? I don't even know how you are involved in this. But you realize that Brian is already looking into your disappearance, and you won't get away with whatever this is, right?"

"Really? We shall see about that. Lily Sweet. Daughter of Adelaide Croy and Charlie Sweet. It's nice to finally see the woman that caused so much trouble for my family."

Adelaide didn't look particularly nervous. In fact, she instead appeared to have gone in a trance.

"Your family? What do you mean, your family?" I asked.

"Lily, Lily. Such a disappointing cousin. Oh! You didn't know? You see, a long time ago, about twenty-five or so, I was adopted at birth by a lovely family named Serrano. However, my birth mother made one tiny mistake when she threw me out like yesterday's trash. She tucked my birth certificate in with the swaddling."

Yolanda looked at me with such venom, yet her face was familiar in a manner to another woman who hated me with a passion. I had several thoughts running through my mind, but it was not Donna whose name I came up with. Donna had been living with Bubba's father, Ross Gunford, over in Hiawassee. But her sister, the promiscuous Deanna Fredricks, fit the bill.

"You're Deanna's daughter, aren't you?"

Yolanda's eyes widened in mild surprise, and she smiled, although it never reached her cold, dead eyes. "Excellent, Lily. Yes. The slut from Sweet Briar, Georgia, was my mother. Now do you see why I'm happy destroying everything you hold dear?"

"No. Not really. This is insanity, Yolanda. I had nothing to do with any of this. Neither did you. You can't blame your family for things they did before you were born. This insane quest for power that you and your aunt and mother are on is just madness!"

"Madness! We share similar blood, Lily Sweet. Maybe you have the madness in you as well? Are you ready to go insane and join me? Who are you to talk, anyway? Everyone is so thrilled to have you back. Do you think your family will welcome the bastard child of a bastard child as one of their own? The high and mighty Dolce clan wouldn't even give my mother and aunt a second look when their magic didn't meet the standards deemed worthy. The Croy clan wouldn't even acknowledge us!"

"But to go after an entire family and try and destroy them won't bring you any happiness. You can't buy love and acceptance, Yolanda."

"I would never have the chance! My mother threw me

away. It wasn't until a few years ago when I met my Aunt Donna that I truly felt I belonged somewhere!"

Yeah, and Donna being a sociopath didn't exactly foster the mindset Yolanda needed.

"I'm sure your adopted family loves you, Yolanda. How can you say that?"

"Loves me? You stupid fool. You know nothing about me. And why would you? The protected little darling. The Serrano family I went into had different ideas about what being a low-level witch meant. I was to go into trade. Earn a living. Do good deeds. I had no choice in anything. Forcing me to take up medicine and working my way up...not get handed everything like you. Even then, it never satisfied my adopted parents. They pushed me and pushed me and were only happy when they could brag about a new position I achieved in the medical world."

"Yolanda, that sounds like what every normal parent hopes for their child... I'm sure..."

"You are sure of nothing!" Yolanda spat, circling to the other side of me away from Adelaide. "You never have to work. You have a trust. You never have to scrimp and save and hope if you climb another rung in the ladder, you can make enough to pay off the loans you took for college, hoping you have enough to pay down the mortgage on a townhouse you can barely afford. You never dream you'd have it easy, like someone who has a house handed to them just because their family is wealthy."

I knew my trying to tell her of the years of poverty, the desperation, and isolation I'd lived through with my mentally ill Aunt Jessica, the days and nights we would go without food, working two jobs and hoping the disability check would arrive in time to pay a rent we couldn't afford would mean anything to this bitter woman.

"Yolanda. People have to make choices in life, and despite

where they have come from or where they are heading, despite who their family is...or isn't, it comes down to what choices you decide. You can be bitter, or you can be grateful. You can choose to be positive or negative. You can choose which path you will take. Don't use the choices your mother made as an excuse to do such hateful things."

"Choice? Do you think I had a choice? If you grow up without love...the love and acceptance you crave, do you think it so easy? What if you do have all the love you can handle? Does it make choosing any easier? Why don't we find out then, shall we?"

With that last question tossed at me in hatred, Yolanda spun around and threw the ball of magic out in front of her. I thought I had felt dread moments before when the Sentinels made their hellish appearance, but what materialized before me terrorized my heart and shocked me to my core. I knew at once, no matter the outcome, today, I would lose something I held dear.

Floating in a suspended state in one gigantic glass dome was Brian Chase, eyes fixed on my face. In another equally huge dome hovered Lorcan, his eyes also gazing at me with such sorrow and longing I thought my heart would break in two. Floating below them was some kind of river made of smoke that twirled and twisted in a labyrinth pattern. At once, I knew I would make a choice that would devastate me.

"Ah. Has the realization hit you yet, my sweet? Yes? Good, good. You must choose one or the other. Who will you free to escape with you to the surface above? Who will be lost to Time, forever wandering the endless puzzle below, without the hope of ever finding freedom...wasting away for centuries until just the memory of his ever having lived will be all that is left to haunt the labyrinth for eternity?"

I looked at Lorcan then over to Brian. I knew they could hear. I saw it in the pleading looks they were both giving me.

Brian's intense and unwavering, almost commanding me to let it be he who would fall to the pit below. Lorcan, sending me a soft loving look that begged not to let his friend die in his stead, that he would gladly suffer this fate to save me and allow Brian his freedom. They both glanced at each other, and I could see they knew the reality of the situation, that one of them would possibly walk out of here with me and the other be doomed.

Damn it all. I was not going to make a choice and let either of these men suffer, nor was I going to let Yolanda waltz out of here, the victor.

I am Lily Sweet, Dark Witch, and I am about to kick some inferior witch butt.

I felt my eyes go dark and my hands crackle with energy. At the same time, I saw Adelaide crumble to the ground and Wicked rushing to stand over her, tail swishing and a low growl rattling out of her. I refused to take my eyes off Yolanda and could only hope that my mother was OK, and pretending to be down or overcome with fatigue and could not stay upright.

Yolanda sneered and raised the circlet high above her head. How did she get that?

"How did you remove the circlet from the pedestal? How were you able to anticipate all this?"

"Why should I indulge you? Oh, very well. Donna told me my mother cursed that circlet. You knew Adelaide meddled in dark arts best left alone, and Deanna might have been an inferior witch, but she had a knack at tampering with spells. When Edith Plank touched that tiny black kitten totem, I knew someone was trying to find the reversal spell. It called to me as the circlet responds to you." She sneered, eyes glowing with malice in the eerie lighting.

"That totem allowed me entrance to these rooms when-ever I wanted, for you see, I have its twin. I can come and go out of this forbidden library at will. I've had this chamber at the ready since I learned the riddle and the cost to reverse the spell. Someone has to give their soul to reverse it. Donna altered it so that instead of the victor falling into hell, it would be the victor's choice. This was easy for me to set up. The minute you touched the totem, I used mine to whisk me here."

"You've been helping Donna. You were the scraggly woman hitching a ride with Harley and gave him the potion that paralyzed him. You were the one to possess Rowan Nightingale with some kind of dark magic. You've been doing so much ruinous stuff to win her approval, haven't you? You realize the woman is mad, right?"

"Correct. But let's not continue our chat. Trying to forestall me or distract me will not work, Lily. I have the circlet and its power. It responds to me. Make your choice now. I'm growing bored and may drop them both into the abyss."

"Do you seriously think I will allow it? That I won't stop you? And that you are the stronger witch?" I scolded.

No matter what item of magic she had in her possession, I wore the rest of the sweetbriar jewelry. I anticipated that my power would call my ancestors, giving me the strength over anything Yolanda believed she possessed.

I made the first strike and watched as a minuscule blip of magic shot out of my fingertips and weakly bounced around the room.

Yolanda threw her head back and howled with laughter.

"Oh, wow. Nora said you were a talentless hack. I didn't believe her and chalked it up to jealousy. But you really do suck at this, don't you?"

"Not really, dear. I was just toying with you." I could see Yolanda smirking, sure of her victory. I counted on her arrogance and the slanderous vitriol Nora had been spreading to work in my favor...and it was. Yolanda didn't need to know I had mastered one particular talent and could call forth a most dreadful spell. I might have an arsenal of dark magic that I could not control yet, but I only needed the one I could command.

My eyes flicked to a spot just beyond where she was standing, and I suddenly felt confident I would get out of this alive, as would my friends and family. Yolanda hadn't noticed the ground behind her go from a slick black floor to an expulsion of earth that was reminiscent of a freshly opened grave. I did, however.

"Toying with me? You must think me a fool."

"No. I know you are a fool. Mortimer here will be witness to that, won't you, Morty?"

Yolanda's brow furrowed in confusion.

"What are you talking about? Stop trying to distract me and fight. I want you to go down in a writhing pile of pain, but not before you see me drop one of your precious beaus into the void. Hmm...I do believe I will set Lorcan free. I can weave a memory spell on him and take him as my lover. I've had Brian...plus, he's so lacking in loyalty, I find him offensive now. Yes...Brian goes down."

"No. He doesn't. It's time for you to eat dirt."

With that, I sent the Imperium Tormentum Mortis curse flying into Yolanda. I knew I'd performed the spell correctly when I saw her face go from surprised to mindless in an instant, then go slack. At the same time, Mortimer opened a hole in the ground, and I watched in fascination as Yolanda Serrano slid into the labyrinth below, not even able to scream out in distress as she passed from this level to the darkness beyond.

Once she disappeared from view, Mortimer sealed the floor. It was over.

"Thank you, Mortimer," I said with a shaky voice.

"You are very welcome, my dear. Imagine my surprise

when I felt my pocket vibrate and realized I still had that tiny contraption your great-grandfather slipped in my pocket when he came to visit me a few months back. Why...I wasn't sure the little trinket would still work in all this time, but buzz away it did until I opened it and found a note from Adriana. Off I rushed just now, worrying I might arrive too late to offer my aid, but...all is well. All is well. I think this is a good spot to take my nap. Would you mind if I took myself off to the other room? I am ever so tired."

"Of course, Mortimer. But first, do you think you can free my friends while I tend to my mother? I don't know what kind of magic Yolanda employed to put them in the glass cases...but, well...surely you could free them or close up that floor?"

"How silly of me not to realize this. Of course, of course. Go see to Adelaide."

I gave the vampire a grateful look as Mortimer began lumbering over to the area where Lorcan and Brian dangled as I rushed to help Adelaide. I'd just reached her when I heard the sickening sound of glass cracking slowly.

Spinning around, I watched in horrified fascination as the dome that held Brian began to chink and split. The pinging and whining reverberations from the glass told us we had seconds to devise a plan to save him from having the same fate as Yolanda.

But just as I called out to Mortimer to do something, the glass shattered, and Brian Chase plummeted to the murky depths below.

I don't remember screaming. I don't remember any sound at all.

I could see Mortimer flash past me and reach down, looking every which way even as Lorcan's glass began to crack. Instead of taking any more time to search for Brian, Mortimer reached up, pulled Lorcan's crystalline prison over to the room we were standing in, and thrust his arms into the glass, making it explode in a million shards. Lorcan was free.

Turning back to where Brian had dropped into the labyrinth, I was gutted to find a floor smooth with no trace of the murky smoke.

"Brian!" I screamed again and again until I felt Lorcan's arms wrap around me.

"No! He can't be gone. We have to save him. We have to! He said his family was cursed. We can't let this be true. We can't!" I kept thinking of the little boy who discovered his father's lifeless body. And sobbed liked I'd never had before.

Despite the empath energy flowing into me from Lorcan, I didn't think my tears would dry up, or I'd ever be happy again.

CHAPTER 20

*O*ne week had passed, and my mother, Adelaide, had lain in a state of slumber in the old master bedroom in my home. The room I knew she secretly shared with my father, Charlie. Almost like Sleeping Beauty, only making the occasional movement or sound to let us know she was well, her eyes would flutter open, then she would smile and drift off once again. Her body needing to heal from the ordeal of being locked inside a cat for twenty-plus years.

Wicked had indeed survived and proved her magical aptitude by not only remaining corporeal and vivacious, but continuing to act like a kitten of three months and not an aged cat of twenty-five years. Her attitude hadn't changed, and if anything, she seemed to get snarkier every day. She was quickly forgiven for her sour cattitude by the very fact that she was my fierce heroine, having chosen to face those ghastly Sentinels, putting her tiny body between them and me, then standing guard over Adelaide.

We still had no answers as to why she or Adelaide protected the sweet briar rose outside my back door or what the poppet means. I had hopes that, once Adelaide had her strength back, she'd enlighten us all. To that and every question we'd ever had.

Olivia had finally resurfaced after being ill for a few days and told me she thought she'd recognized the last name, Serrano. They were a family of witches from North Carolina that had asked the Council to push their daughter up the ranks landing her a position as the medical examiner in Gwinnett. They hoped it would settle their 'troubled' daughter, who never seemed to be satisfied with anything in life. You'd think that would have raised some alarm bells in the Council. Again, confirming I had every right to question their abilities.

Mortimer had put off his slumber to excavate the forbidden library, his daily excursions to the bottomless depths a testament to his not giving up on finding Brian and freeing him from an unjust prison. With Yolanda as the soul needed, I, the victor, chose to fall into that hell below. Brian's wasn't bound there.

Rita Chase waited on news, daily, standing outside the bottom of a small cliff where a hole had been bored into its base. Under Susanne's Methodist Church, Mortimer was making a new entry where debris and detritus could be sorted, and any nasty creatures that might try and escape from below were trapped and whisked off by the Council.

Yeah. The Council.

They finally got around to conceding to the wishes of my family. I guess having a marginally competent witch like Yolanda fly under their radar and causing such havoc had sent some heads spinning and made the Elders realize some things had to change or our way of life would crumble.

I spent the last three days standing by Rita's side, bringing her foodstuffs from my Uncle Stephen's café. She never ate.

She never moved. She just watched the hole and waited as the trackers went in and out, aiding Mortimer on his quest. Seeing as I was, in fact, a tracker myself, I had demanded to be let in and try to assist in the recovery—I refused to consider calling it anything else. However, as yet untrained in my talent, I needed to allow those better suited to do what needed doing—basically, I was asked not to get in their way. Tracing spells was one thing...looking for a soul, another.

Adriana arrived today and mumbled some incantations around the opening, then joined us at our observation post.

"Any word?" I asked.

"Only that Mortimer seems to think Brian may have been muddled and doesn't understand which way he is heading, not believing any calls or sounds of rescue, but instead staying trapped in whatever horror Yolanda had cast as his fate." Rita had tears streaming down her face at these words, and I wrapped my arms around her shoulders, offering comfort. "We will find him, Rita. Don't give up hope." Adriana patted her back.

Suddenly I felt a sense of overwhelming calm come over me and knew Lorcan was nearby. Turning, I saw him walk toward us. And he came to a stop on the other side of me he clasped my hand. Rita glanced down, noting our fingers entwined, smiling thinly, then returned her gaze to the black cavern in front of us. At least she seemed happy for Lorcan and me, but I had to wonder if she wished it were Lorcan we were searching for instead of her son.

Suddenly, we heard a massive explosion, and the ground shook, leaving us breathless in alarm. Before we could react, we saw Mortimer burst forth from the gaping hole, Brian, secure in his arms. At least, we thought it was Brian. It looked more like a giant monster holding a raven-haired Ken Doll in his grasp.

Turning his head and spying our small congregation on the hill, Mortimer changed his route and loped our way in one giant forward motion. Gently, for such a vast and powerful vampire, Mortimer placed a pale and sickly-looking Brian at his crying mother's feet.

"He's back! He's, oh my gosh. Will he be ok? Brian...please wake up. Please!" I was crying along with Rita while Adriana spoke softly with Mortimer, walking away from us a short distance. When she had finished, she returned and placed her arm around Rita, assuring her that all would be well. Mortimer returned to the opening, and even as I watched, I could see him seal himself and the opening up, blocking the way to the labyrinth beyond...and ending this nightmare.

Lorcan was smiling in relief and stood beside Rita, who was cradling her son's head in her lap, her tears wetting his face and smearing the soot into runny grayish trails down his face. Brian seemed ok but was gaunt and withdrawn and didn't seem to be able to regain consciousness.

I could hear the sirens in the distance and saw Shirley Jones in her EMT vehicle heading our way before the rest of my party. The sheriff and a firetruck were right behind them. How odd to see the ordinary after what we'd been through. It almost seemed incongruous to have an ambulance arrive to save the day. Although, deep inside, I knew they were magical first responders on the scene. Still, I was having difficulty with the paranormal versus the mundane right now.

After a bit of working on Brian and getting him on a stretcher, Shirley and her team were ready to transport him to the hospital. Rita joined her son in the back of the ambulance as Shirley got instructions from a Council Elder nearby on where to take him. Adriana fell behind with me and Lorcan, a smile on her aged face.

"Will he be ok?" I asked her.

"I think so. He's back. Brian out of that hell. That's a good thing. What his brain has suffered can only be determined by a team of Clerics. That's where he is heading now. To the specialized hospital wing. I told Rita not to fret over the cost...our family will take care of it."

I nodded gratefully at my great-grandmother and leaned into Lorcan, who had his arms open and ready to embrace me. Adriana glanced at the two of us and smiled, then addressed me.

"I didn't have time to tell you since you returned, what with settling Adelaide and dealing with the hundreds of relatives that tried to come to invade your home and get a gander at her, but you did good, squirt. Real good. I knew you could do that curse. I taught you well."

"You did not teach me how to control that spell! Tanaquil did!"

"A minor detail. The fact of the matter is, you, my dear, are one mighty dark witch."

"And don't you forget it, old lady. Don't you forget it."

* * *

FIVE DAYS after Brian's rescue, we received word that he was recovering albeit slowly. The clerics had not yet measured the damage to his brain, but he was waking up in dribs and drabs and seemed to be aware he was home and safe. They only allowed Rita to see him, and she'd reported that he recognized her at least. We took this as a win.

We had to.

Brian chose to fight alongside me in a battle he didn't have to fight. He was a hero as far as I was concerned.

So was the big lug that was ready to give his life for his

one-time friend. I suspected they would once again be friends—the rift mended.

Right now, we were trying to get things back to normal and go on with our lives. We still had many questions, but for now, they could wait. We had time.

Lorcan had spent the last few days coming over, tilling up the little patch of ground I'd slated for my garden spot. It was about one week too late to be planting my peas as far as Donald Murphy was concerned, but I'd go ahead and see what would come of it.

Lorcan was grumbling at my choice for the garden plot. At first, he insisted I would want to place it over by the sunniest spot in my tiny yard. However, I informed him I had it on good authority the area I chose would be perfect. Shaking his head but accepting my decree, he began tilling in earnest until I had a lovely little patch complete with the new pea seeds interred, awaiting the signal to sprout into tiny pea vines.

"I hope you know what you are talking about. This spot seems awful shady."

"It doesn't matter."

"No?"

"No." I smiled then gave Lorcan a hug breathing in his manly scent, a heady combination of pine and bergamot and the dirt he'd been plowing, with a hint of sweat.

"Ok, smarty pants. What happens when this spot doesn't give enough sunlight and your plants wither?" He asked.

"Lily will use that newfound magic of hers and order them plants to grow, she will."

"Abner! Will you get out of my potting shed and go away...please?"

Abner shrugged and ambled off in the direction of Main Street and turned north toward the town. Lorcan and I just shook our heads, watching him go, then laughed at my annoying but beloved fixture of a handyman. A label Abner informed us he had been tasked with by the previous owners —my parents. That explained the set of keys he had and his ability to come and go with ease.

"I know it might be out of line, what with Brian still not out of the woods and everything in a flux, but seeing as today happens to be Valentine's Day, I brought you something."

Valentine's Day!

Oh *no*. I had completely forgotten and hadn't been even thinking about such things. I had nothing to give Lorcan in return, and he immediately saw the chagrin cross my face.

"Hold on, Tink." Calling me by the nickname he'd given me because of my fondness for the little Disney fairy and the fact I put found items together as I tinkered in my art studio. Lorcan began to explain.

"First of all, you just made me a whirligig for the roof of my mechanic shop...and you refused to let me pay you. Then you made an intricate and incredible bird feeder sculpture thingy for my mom and dad's yard. The neighbors are still talking about it. It's a work of art! So, stop right there before you worry that you hadn't given me anything.

You've given me so much more than any gift you could purchase or make. You gave me hope. Hope that I could have the life I dreamed about but never thought possible. So just forget whatever it is you have going on in that brain of yours. Today it's all about us. I'm taking you out to dinner tonight, on a proper date. Here."

With those last words, Lorcan reached into his jacket and pulled out a file. On it was a big red stamp that stated: Cancelled, removed from the registry.

Daring not to believe what he handed me but bubbling with glee that only my Lorcan would understand, I reached for it. This would be better than any trinket he could have bought for this lovers' holiday. I opened the file to find the long-held banns of marriage between one Lorcan Reid and one Nora Haywood removed from the Tribunal registry. No longer was he tied to my cousin, and we were free to announce to the world we were an item.

"Lily Sweet. My beautiful dark witch. I don't know where we are heading just yet, but I can't imagine my life without you." Lorcan reached for my hand and dropped a tiny charm onto my palm. It was a platinum heart, with my Pisces symbol on one half, and a Cancer symbol...Lorcan's sign, on the other. It would look perfect next to the sweet briar rose charm dangling on the bracelet I always wore. I had already added the tiny Pisces charm my father had given to me, and now it looks like I had a third. This also explained the trip to the jewelry store.

"Oh, Lor...I love it. Thank you! It's darling. I feel the same way about us too. Somehow, I finally think things are moving in the right direction, and we are getting the answers we need to put all this drama behind us and start our lives."

"Once Adelaide can fully awaken and tell us the details we are missing and hopefully bring your father home," Lorcan said.

I knew we still had a long road ahead of us with battles and unmentionable dark magic heading our way. But with Adelaide back and my strength as a witch growing and my friends and family around me, I felt like we could accomplish anything we set our minds to.

"Yes. Once Adelaide is fully awake. Then we can tackle that problem like we've done the others—and we will win. I just know it." Lorcan smiled down at me, then opened his arms again, and for the next few moments, no words were necessary.

That is, until a searing pain slammed into my head, tearing and shredding at the delicate skin on my scalp.

Lorcan, too, suffered the attack, and we both cried out in dismay, trying to free ourselves from our tormentor.

"Wicked! Oh...you horrible, ungrateful, diabolical fiend. Just wait, cat, I will shave you bald and make mittens out of your fur. I'm going to make you wish you'd never been...*gah!*"

* * *

THANK YOU FOR READING! I hope you loved meeting Lily and Lorcan, and the rest of the characters. The next book in the Lily Sweet Mysteries is Revenge is Sweet, Witch. Find out if Adelaide will recover and tell Lily and the family what happened all those years ago to cause them to run in fear. Does she know who is behind all of the evil attacks on the family?

CLICK HERE TO READ REVENGE IS SWEET, NOW>

And if you enjoyed Witch Way Did He Go?, you'll love Maggie and her quirky, sometimes funny, sometimes dark, but always magical paranormal gang of monster-hunting antique appraisers. A Tale of Two Sisters, the tie-in series to my Lily Sweet World, highlights Lily's cousins Maggie and Ellie Fortune and is FREE on Kindle Unlimited!

"I am loving the snark in this book."

- S. Keller, BookBub author reviews.

I appreciate your help in spreading the word, including telling friends and family. Reviews help readers find books! Please leave a review on your favorite book site.

You can also join my Facebook Group: Author Bettina M. Johnson's Team Wicked for exclusive giveaways and sneak peek of future books—and just plain silliness!

SIGN UP FOR BETTINA M. JOHNSON'S NEWS-LETTER: http://eepurl.com/gZKo51

Continue on for a short excerpt from Revenge is Sweet, Witch....

Revenge is Sweet, Witch

"Why isn't she waking up?"

I fussed with the coverlet, tucking it around my mother, Adelaide Croy Sweet, to ward off the chill, even though our temperatures here in Sweet Briar, Georgia, had been steadily improving. I was amazed to see daffodils and forsythia making an appearance in my garden—something that would not happen in the Catskill Mountains of New York State, where I lived most of my life—for another two months, if then.

I'd just recently found out the woman who was in a perpetual slumber in her old bedroom in the house I had inherited was, in fact, my mother and not my aunt. It was a very long and sordid tale involving evil witches, my parents, and my aunt concealing the structure of their relationship and the verity behind my birth, along with so many unanswered questions which resulted in murder, mayhem, and a mystery I had yet to solve.

Trying to help me solve this puzzle was my great-grandmother, Adriana Dolce. My father, Charlie's grandmother, and the matriarch of our family. Don't let the fact that she is a centenarian fool you—Granny is a hellion in a cape and pointy hat, a dark witch like me, and the average Joe would be crazy to cross her path with anything but the utmost respect.

Oh, yes, witches. We were a rather large and prolific family—the Dolce's and Croy's—to name a few of the surnames that made up my crazy clan. Some of that mayhem I mentioned could very well be our fault. Using spells and magic always came with a price, as I just recently found out. My name is Lily Sweet, the aforementioned dark witch, which does not mean I do evil things. It's more like I am one asshat away from letting my magic loose and protecting the innocent or seeking justice for those wronged.

"That is what the Clerics are trying to figure out, Squirt. That and why she went under so deeply in the first place." Adriana was a formidable dark witch, keen on getting to the bottom of this family's afflictions and hellbent on taking on the matter of one, Donna Fredricks. Granny wanted to throttle her until she spilled all the secrets that she'd been keeping from us.

I just wanted to throttle her because of all the vile things she'd enacted upon my family.

I was beyond frustrated and impatient. When I first freed my mother from her sentence of being bound to my cat Wicked—a nasty spell had them fused for the last twenty-one years with Adelaide stuck inside my cat—I was sure my mother would have all the answers to the questions that had been haunting my family for years. And thought, great, now we will learn everything!

But, yet again, I had to learn to be patient, seeing as how she had been sleeping now going on two and a half weeks with only the occasional eye flutterings and smiles to let us know she wasn't in any dire predicaments. While it was unusual for a patient to be out so long, the witch Clerics informed us that the extraordinary circumstances around Adelaide's decades-long furry prison could be the reason for such a lengthy recovery.

"Try to be patient, cara. Adelaide will come around when she can. She knows we need those answers."

That was all well and good. However, I wasn't a very patient person.

"Plus, we have other pressing matters to attend. I want to hit that lower level of the prison, despite Mortimer's dire warnings, before the Witch Council decides to grow a back-bone and blows the place to smithereens!"

Mortimer Snodgrass was a vampire who aided us in recent weeks. And despite any preconceived notions you may carry are regarding the bloodsuckers, old Morty was a good egg, even if he did warn us not to enter the witch prison.

Wait a minute. We were what?

* * *

SOCIAL MEDIA LINKS

I write in my own style that may not be everyone's cup of tea —so if you enjoy my characters and humor, my plots, how the storyline is developing, etc. and are eagerly anticipating the next in the series, be aware that I am just as excited as you are—I've found someone who thinks my story ideas are neat! That is thrilling for any writer to know (or it should be). THANK YOU!

Visit my official website to receive updates, find out about special offers and new releases, or read my blog about writing and farm life - complete with photos - you might even catch me mowing my ten acres (seriously): http://www.bettinamjohnson.net

For more information or to contact me:
author@bettinamjohnson.net

For even more (if you just can't enough of me) follow my
Social Media Links

Mailing List - https://bit.ly/2BvQXmP
BookBub - https://bit.ly/2Epejwj
Goodreads - https://bit.ly/3aTejQW
Author Page - Amazon - https://amzn.to/3lj7L2L
Instagram - https://bit.ly/2QpZa01
TikTok - https://bit.ly/2PQa6Hg
MeWe - https://bit.ly/36A2RcM
Facebook - https://bit.ly/3gOaFZY
Twitter: https://bit.ly/3jahMgY
YouTube - https://bit.ly/2Stvy2X

ABOUT THE AUTHOR

I always knew I wanted to write. As a kid, way before the technology age had hit, I'd be stuck in the car with the folks as we drove from our home on Staten Island, NY, where I was born and raised, to our family property in the Catskill Mountains. To drive away boredom, I would sit, staring out the window, and create adventures of daring thieves riding horseback along the road, trying to escape the law. Other times I'd imagine a wild girl riding her unicorn into battle (I had a vivid imagination - we didn't have video games yet!).

As the years passed, I'd start writing a book, then stop, then start again only to let life get in the way, until one day I had an epiphany—a kick in the pants moment. If I waited any longer, all those wonderful characters in my head would never have their stories told, and that made me sad. So, I treated writing as my career. Once I started, it became apparent nothing would ever stop me again. YOU, dear reader, are stuck with me until I go off to that great library in the sky...or wherever writers go when they crumble to dust in front of their typewriters (or laptops...whatever!).

I live in the North Georgia mountains on what I like to call a farm, with my husband and almost adult kids, a Cairn Terrier, a bunch of cats, and fish. Occasionally other critters show up to keep things exciting.

BOOKS BY BETTINA M. JOHNSON

The Lily Sweet Mysteries:

Home Sweet Witch

Witch Way is Up?

How To Train Your Witch

Sweet Home Liliana

Witch Way Did He Go?

Revenge is Sweet, Witch

The Sweet Spell of Success (Coming Soon)

* * *

The Fortune-Telling Twins Mysteries:

A Tale of Two Sisters

Double Toil and Trouble (Coming Soon)